BORN LOSERS

BARBARA SKELTON

Born Losers

SHORT STORIES

faber and faber

This edition first published in 2008
by Faber and Faber Ltd
3 Queen Square, London WC1N 3AU

Printed by Books on Demand GmbH, Norderstedt

All rights reserved
© Barbara Skelton, 1965

The right of Barbara Skelton to be identified as author of this work
has been asserted in accordance with Section 77 of the
Copyright, Designs and Patents Act 1988

This book is sold subject to the condition that it shall not, by way of
trade or otherwise, be lent, resold, hired out or otherwise circulated
without the publisher's prior consent in any form of binding or cover other than
that in which it is published and without a similar condition including this
condition being imposed on the subsequent purchaser

A CIP record for this book is available from the British Library

ISBN 978–0–571–24831–5

Our authorised representative in the EU for product safety is
Easy Access System Europe, Mustamäe tee 50, 10621 Tallinn, Estonia
gpsr.requests@easproject.com

Contents

Orphan of Manhattan	1
Born Losers	14
Count on Me	29
A Wet Cherry Bomb	46
The Square	54
Dorothy, Get Yourself Analysed	67
Gloomsville	83
What's New?	94
Nutty as a Fruit Cake	105
Sour Grapes	120
This is the Life	131
How Much Longer?	139

Orphan of Manhattan

I was going to have a wonderful time in New York, everyone said. 'It is London with a shot of cocaine.' The least enthusiastic were always women. From England I wrote to friends asking if it were possible to find a furnished apartment. One wrote back jubilantly claiming to know of a duplex, she couldn't recommend it, though, the kitchen looked on to Puerto Ricans. Another wrote, 'Think I have found you a place. Fifth Avenue. Splendid address. Owned by a wild living honey round forty.' 'Divorced' was added in brackets, as if announcing a trade. When everything was settled the honey wired cancelling the arrangement. So I booked into a hotel on E. 56th St. A very good location! Rooms from 28 to 35 dollars a week.

'They treat you like cattle in those cheap hotels.' 'They're all brothels in that area.' 'Twenty-eight dolls a day more likely,' someone else said. I had been warned of the slow Economy flight, with no place to stretch your legs. 'If you're not in a hurry, why fly and arrive a wreck? Better take a rest on a boat.' 'Don't take the boat,' said the little travel agent, 'these days, even if you share a cabin, it costs more than going by air. It's the tipping that counts.' So a jet was decided on. 'They won't give you anything to eat, but you'll get your fill of drink,' the travel man concluded.

The last evening the telephone was very busy, everybody was anxious to pass on the names of people they knew in the States. An old friend came round expressly to claim a book I had borrowed; when he heard I was planning to be away for three months on 1,000 dollars, after a flicker of envy I should even possess such a sum, he said crabbily, 'You'll last ten days on that.' Heeding the travel agent's warning at the airport I took the precaution of eating a high tea of smoked trout and chops. The take-off was at 5 p.m. 'Don't expect any help with your luggage on arrival,' were the words of farewell from a friend. During the flight two meals were brought, both of which, as though they might be the last, driven on by thrift, I ate. When not eating, on the advice of the steward I stretched out on the vacant seats and slept, to arrive six hours later, New York dinner time. In the customs I grabbed a trolley pram, piled on the luggage and wheeled up to one of the queues. In the gallery above, Q, looking like a washed out greyhound buttoned in a pale camel overcoat, stood waving. He beckoned to the main hall where he greeted me with:

'Want a taxi cab? If so, it'll cost you 10 dollars.' We boarded the bus and I said:

'What happened to the girl you came here to marry?'

'Her husband died. It changed everything. Here men die off right, left and centre. Women are two a penny.' Q's hand swept through my handbag for a cigarette and he remarked on the wad of introductions.

'By all means send them off. You'll be asked out once and you'll think you're getting on like a house on fire. Suddenly you never get a peek out of anyone again. You're left wondering what hit you.'

Ten-foot mounds of snow were stacked against the kerb and shovellers were piling it into disposal trucks before a thaw flooded the city. It was far colder than London. At the hotel on E. 56th St. there was no porter. The girl at the desk handed us the key and Q dragged the cases into the elevator. On the tenth floor we squeezed along a passage smelling of vegetable fry. The narrow room was filled with a divan that had two threadbare blankets; the grey-painted side table and dressing table were coated in black dust; the heat was overwhelming; it was impossible to turn off the hissing hot pipes, adjust the broken Venetian blind, open the window or for more than one person to circuit the room; we remained standing at the door and discussed where to eat as an occasional cockroach nuzzled along the floorboard and plaster flaked from the ceiling on our heads.

Of the first nine introductions, one woman politely replied to say her father had just died and she hoped she'd see me on my next visit. A publisher rang and asked, how was it I was still in? Shouldn't I be out rubber-necking? Finally, he said, 'When you're at a loose end call me. If I should ever have any time I'll call you.' There was further contact. Another rang anxious to know if my London flat would be available for his pending visit to Europe. When told it was occupied, he hung up. I did not hear again. Another was leaving for Germany. A fifth telephoned to invite me for a drink two weeks ahead. The only other reaction came many weeks later; a strange man called and offered me a part in a forthcoming musical, there was just one part left for an English girl. I'd been recommended by so-and-so (one of the introductions). How lucky I was still available. Half-way through the plot I interrupted to explain his mistake. He sounded genuinely disappointed.

It did not take long to discover that even in the scruffiest bar, one of the main pleasures of New York are the drinks. From large cartons of 100 per cent pure unsweetened King Sun fruit juice to large iced martinis, Rob Roys (a Martini made with Scotch) and Red Snappers (Bloody Mary made with gin) named after a Florida fish. The alcohol content in a bottle of whisky is 86 per cent. I became wary of ordering wine, after hearing many a joyous waiter's peal of, 'Another dago red here.' A Beaujolais bottle is treated like a skittle, passed from one attendant to the next and finally presented for you to finger and pronounce that it's hot enough. Red wine by the glass can be good drunk like a Martini, iced with a slice of lemon and brought on a paper doily mat, known as a coaster, which protects the furniture from condensation.

One gets used to seeing large parties of very young girls in black dresses and pearls clustering into night clubs as though just disgorged from a charabanc. The most prominent table in the room is reserved for them. One is never bored for lack of incident, like a harmless scene in a jazz club with a waiter who will try to charge for six beers when you had four.

'I think you've made a mistake. We only had four,' you will point out.

'Six beers,' he will stress, and with an accusing leer. 'Yer mean to say yer been here all this time and only had four beers?'

'We haven't been here that long.'

'You had six beers alright,' and leering again, 'Do yer want me to be out of pocket. I'll have ter make up the loss.' You nudge your way through the congested bar where shorn-headed men sit in a state of torpor with just sufficient zeal to thrust their glasses forward for replenishment, while others stand behind them swinging backwards and forwards on their heels, fixedly staring ahead and downing their drinks with dedicated precision, as though pressed for time to swallow. At the door the proprietor will be intercepting each departing victim with 'Enjoyed your evening?'

'Clip joint,' you say irritably. 'Funny waiters you have here. They overcharged us.'

'That's it!' The proprietor nods and beams with understanding. 'That's it!' he cries. 'You gotta watch 'em. You just gotta watch 'em.'

Once more we are out in the windy icy street with its flapping drifts of used newspapers, crunching our way over the rinds, stubs and squashed cartons, each with a hand clapped against an eye, in an unsuccessful attempt to ward off the gusts of grit. We stop a cabman and demand to see a burlesque show. 'All been cleaned up,' he says, 'since five years now.' We ask why. 'They were too damned filthy.' 'Like the streets maybe. It's a pity there isn't a bit more cleaning up outside as well as in in this city.'

Back in the hotel lobby an argument is going on between two policemen and the porter, which abates as I enter the lift. I fall asleep and am woken shortly after by the sound of raised voices outside the door. The porter's tone soars to a frenzied animal wail. 'Stop yellin'! Stop yellin'!' he bawls, 'the police is comin'.'

'They're taking a long time coming,' says a man.

'She's undesirable,' cries another man, 'I'm going to have her out.'

'I dare say. But I happen to love her.'

'I'm different from you. I come from the West Indies. Why don't you be a gentleman?'

'Keep your hands off me.'

'Why don't you go home. I don't want no trouble,' screams the porter, 'the police is comin'.' Voices continued for an hour. In the morning the same porter appeared with the usual carton of mud coffee. What had it all been about?

'Some silly man,' he says, 'called in the police to worry that poor ole lady in number seven. Silly man! Tryin' to get in her room, and behavin' as he was married to her. And she nearly blind too. But the poor ole thing. She just couldn't be bothered.'

'Well, what's happened now?'

'Oh, now,' he spoke with infinite satisfaction, 'now everything's quite alright. She's got somebody else up dere.' Late that morning I passed through the hall. The manager looked up from the reception desk. Joyfully, he cried, 'My! You're looking tired. Been up all night?' When the month terminated he tried to persuade me to keep on the room.

'We like having you here,' he said, 'you seem like a nice little lady with a nice disposition. But I suppose you gotta live with them to know.'

'Well, it depends how you treat them.'

'You've been treated well enough here, haven't you? Just like one of the family.'

Some people in Europe share the notion that out of veneration Americans cherish their women and that New York is a haven for women. Of the two recognizable types of American man, one appears to have succumbed quite happily to female domination; he is seen daily on the sidewalk wheeling baby's pram. I am more familiar with the 'Touchy Rebel' who interprets the slightest feminine request or assertion of will as a threat to his manhood. Every woman is a ball crusher. He is obsessed with proving his virility which he attempts through an endless conquest of women. One boasted, 'I can even manage the old ones.' The 'Touchy Rebel' seems sub-human with his negation of feeling, a granite-hearted little boy who considers any further emotional commitment will complete his castration. 'Extrication' is a prominent word in his vocabulary. His dominant fear is being trapped. Again, that is. He has been through several marriages, until in a final state of rebellion he at last achieves emancipation in his fifties. He is a victim of passivity and he prefers his women to take the initiative. Along comes the aggressive woman who gradually takes over. This can be his downfall. There he is in the noose again.

The 'Touchy Rebel', being very much in demand in such a female-ridden city, has become extremely spoilt and selfish. He is most engaging as well, his solicitous manner clothes a ferment of hostility released at any hint of criticism of himself or his country. Never suggest that Scotch beef is superior to American. An incredulous stare is followed by an outburst of indignation.

If it means going out of his way he will rarely drop you home, but will shed you on a Park Avenue kerb with the words, 'Call you next week, honey.' This means any time in the far future. 'Call you tomorrow' might mean next week, but 'Call you later' spells never. The most common usage is 'Call me.' This is what he is accustomed to. He will not commit himself to a date ahead, if you are called it's at the last moment, when he's given up hope of an invitation. Don't mention a party to which he has not been asked, it might blight the evening. He will question his friends as to the impression you made. 'She's got a rather mean look,' some woman friend might observe. Then woebetide you. In future it's furtive little dinners served in his apartment. He's learnt to be very self-sufficient in the kitchen. Cramped in a serving pantry he can run up one or two really edible dishes and likes to clean up after them. He serves faultless scrambled eggs. He may wish to see himself as a slob, but is vain of his appearance. Once he has come to terms with what suits him he fancies himself in a phantasy type hat, such as a deerstalker, a yachting cap or a straightforward Stetson. He lacks malice as well as a very high standard of criticism. His intelligence goes in to being good at his job. All 'Touchy Rebels' crave love and attention.

Mr Right is even more elusive in New York; anybody seeking him can spare themself the trouble of crossing the ocean. Apart from the conquest seekers most drifting heterosexuals undergo treatment, but it is possible to catch one in between his self-imposed sessions in a mental home and spend quite a blissful few months. Many are alcoholics. Alcoholism is always referred to with great tact. After a party if someone should inquire how you liked his friend and you say, 'Very much. But he wasn't making much sense, was he?' With a grin, the response is, 'Oh, sure! So and so likes his drink.' This can mean he passes out every night. The morning after an enjoyable evening's drinking, if you should ring and ask how somebody is feeling, the reply invariably is, 'I woke up a little tired, thank you.' The less guilt afflicted will blatantly state, 'I'm already on to Miltowns,' as 'I was absolutely stewed again last night.'

Is A.A. for you?
Do you require a drink the next morning?
Do you prefer to drink alone?
Do you lose time from work due to drinking?
Has drinking changed your personality?
Are you harder to get along with since drinking?
Do you crave a drink at a definite time daily?
Have you thought less of your husband or wife since drinking?
Is drinking clouding your reputation?

If you answered YES to one of these test questions, there is a definite warning that you may be an alcoholic. If you answered Yes to any two, the chances are that you are an alcoholic. If you answered Yes to any three, you definitely are.

Q's reaction was to ask me to accompany him to the nearest A.A. meeting. We hurried in a taxi to the Church of the Heavenly Rest. In the bowels of the church a large hall was filled with expectant faces turned toward a platform where banners hung with slogans of, 'But for the Grace of God', 'Easy Does It', 'First Things Comes First', 'Live and Let Live'. Like any fresh initiate we slunk to the back row seats. The atmosphere was of pleasurable anticipation; chain-smoking ladies in little net doily hats spotted with velvet ribbons, were dressed as if for a cocktail party. There were four guest speakers. As each one reached the rostrum he announced, 'I am an alcoholic.' There followed a minute's respectful silence. 'We are here to stay sober. To help others attain sobriety and to share our experiences with those who desire to stop drinking.' Then each speaker proceeded to describe his first symptoms of 'neurotic compulsion', 'the upchucks', 'loss of friends', 'loss of job' and 'final ego deflation', until having reached 'rock bottom', when both the head shrinker and the doctor had failed, help had been sought through A.A. Women spoke in a tone of sincere religious repentance, the men were more anecdotal and exhibitionist. During the course of the confessions an initiate would reel into the hall, slump into the nearest seat and rumble off to sleep.

Towards the end of the meeting an old lady in a cherry laden picture hat came and sat beside us. She was not interested in the speakers; she wanted to talk herself. In answer to a question about drinking, she maintained she'd never smoked or touched a drink in her life. 'Then what are you doing here?' 'Oh!' she exclaimed, surprised that we shouldn't have guessed, 'But this is MY church.'

With the last speaker off the rostrum, everyone rose for the Lord's Prayer. A plate was being passed round. Would we lend her five cents? She reached over and dropped our coin on the pile. The meeting disbanded. Everybody trooped to an adjoining room where free coffee and buns were served. 'Do you think she's an alcoholic?' 'Well,' Q replied, 'if she is she's certainly not letting on about it.'

A short while after the meeting he called me very late one night. He sounded desperate and was having 'panics', he said. I advised him to get in touch with A.A. He had, but they couldn't be bothered. All they wanted was his money. Would I lend him 100 dollars to be hospitalized. They wouldn't look at him, otherwise. A fine institution! He wanted help now. This instant. He was going to die. The last time I saw him he'd been knocked down by a cab driver and had a black eye. A blackie too, he said. Just imagine that happening in London. All he wanted was to get out of this rat hole. He palmed back the wisps on his prematurely balding egg-shaped head, paid the bill and tottered out of the bar to leave me sitting there. A.A. would consider he had a long way to go before reaching 'final ego deflation' and until he had they were not prepared to waste any time. They can detect at once if a person really wants to be cured.

When the money ran out I obtained a security card and joined the streams of job-seekers who were profiting from the Christmas shopping rush. Every personnel department had a continuous horde. Every day queues of men and women were filling forms to get temporary work. Many a forlorn ageing saleslady had to puzzle over her school data, each detail of which had to be entered, with social and business references. Accepted by a firm of booksellers on Fifth Avenue, I joined the temporary staff attending a full day course of instruction with pay, on how to use a cash register, the mechanics of making a sale and how to develop a plus sales technique. 'Never assume a customer's buying potential is exhausted by one sale.' How you must avoid extremes of dress, that the customer should be greeted pleasantly with the time of day. When he makes a purchase ask if he would like it wrapped. The telephone had to be answered with, 'Merry Christmas from Doubleday'.

The salary was 45 dollars a week, minus the insurance, with a bonus of another 10 dollars a week, only on completion of the six-week sentence. It required seven hours of standing a day, but for a ten-minute break morning and afternoon. Each time the head of the department caught you leaning against one of the book piles he'd bark, 'Come along now, none of that.' Women customers were usually prying for etiquette books, or would peruse the cook books for hours, memorize a recipe, and go away empty handed. 'Can I help you, Madam?' 'Just browsing, thank you,' was the stock reply. 'People don't seem to be spending so much this year. Even less than last,' a regular salesman observed, after we'd been standing all morning without a sale, posted by the swing door beside a best selling stack entitled *Poems for the John*.

At the end of the day buses were crammed with exhausted dozing shoppers slumped over their packages. I would join the surge along Fifth Avenue's kerb, lined with Bowery bums profiting from the Christmas campaign. Rigged as Santa Claus, each one braved the icy winds as he stood swinging a censer to attract the shoppers into the big stores to buy up the bunting displays. On Madison Avenue, no matter the time or weather, a gaping crowd was always gathered outside one of the large banks where a bevy of pretty girls with bare arms and bunting-trimmed ballet skirts, each one clasping the next one's shoulder, would be spinning round the main hall on roller skates.

I did not remain in the book trade long enough to claim any bonus. An advertisement in the *New York Times* took me to another firm on Fifth Avenue to apply as a junior model. There were more queues. More forms had to be filled. I was the last in the file. I reduced my age by ten years and was sent to be vetted by the Medical Board. 'Have you been tested for lumps?' asked the nurse. 'What about fits? And allergies? Which of those do you have? When did you last have mumps?' Finally, she said, 'We can't insist, but would you take a polio injection at once? Also, we need a test of your urine.'

About twenty salesgirls haunted the floor of the Junior Miss Department, their ages ranged from forty to sixty-five and some of them had been with the firm since it was founded. All had varicose veins and were determined to be friendly. Each time I caught an eye of one of them she'd smile, it became a strain each day returning twenty smiles so many times over. It was sale time. None of us were allowed off our feet. With my rictus smile I'd furtively lean against the glass counter of the Better Hats, little net skull caps dotted with velvet bows and ribbons, wait for the hostess to take a coffee break and then volunteer for her chair. The hostess sat in the middle of the floor and answered questions like, 'Do you have anything in toast or pumpkin for my wife?' I'd call over one of the smiling salesladies, it gave one something to do to memorize their names. If a salesgirl thought it time she made a sale, she'd line up behind the desk to grab the next customer. Pointing out any celebrity, one of them would say, while nodding toward a lined lady in drainpipe trousers and an old raincoat, 'There's Katharine Hepburn, isn't she just darling?'

Sometimes to embarrass me one of my friends would come in and hover about the rails pretending to seek a bargain.

Miss Eric was head of the department. Nobody ever got a smile out of her. 'Now then, watch your step,' she'd say, every time she passed and saw my legs comfortably screwed into a corkscrew under the hostess table 'Watch how Doris does it. She's more refined, you know.' I'd wait for Miss Eric to go to lunch and sneak to the airless, cramped model room to read a paper. My absence would soon be noted. A head would appear round the door and a smiling salesgirl say, 'Have you coasted today yet dear?' Dressed in one of the new spring models and a hat dangling with price labels, I'd get in the lift and tour the other floors, lingering a long time in the antique department, as it never had any customers. One day Miss Eric said, 'Your hair! I've never seen anything like it. Go to the Beauty Salon at once and get it teased.' Another time she barked, 'How often do I have to remind you to put on your pancake. Look sharp for goodness sake put on some eyelashes. Watch your step.' I left the same week.

From there I became an assistant to a prosthodontist. He was a dedicated dentist with no sense of time. A kind of saint. He would arrange for a nervous patient to be drugged by his analyst in advance. Once in the chair we'd work on the patient until ten at night, filing down each tooth to a vicious little spike. 'Now then, head on,' the saint would shout above the sound of the high-speed drill, as dressed in a white uniform and sneakers I tried to master a large squirt which filled the victim's mouth with warm water to keep the gums from ignition. I learnt how to tie a bib nicely round the patien's neck and swab the face as eddies of tooth shavings dribbled down on to his clothing. Those who did not need to be drugged were handed a mirror. It was considered therapeutic to be able to see what was happening. Fifteen-minute breaks were devoted to everyone's drinking coffee and foaming malted milk.

'Thank you, nurse,' some kind relative would say at the end of the day, when we helped the wreck into a taxi. Green and haggard the saint and I would slowly revive on slugs of whisky. But the patient never looked the same. 'We made a nice job there,' the prosthodontist would say reflectively studying a completed job, while the woman gaped at her new desperate sunken look. I began to have nightmares, convinced I was the next victim. And beginning to detect the dissatisfied expression that all my employers wore sooner or later, I moved on.

I go from one job to the other, from looking after spoilt children and old ladies and hauling them out of the bath, to reading every edition of the Suzy and Knickerbocker column. There's never any trouble finding work. Seventeen pages of employment agencies are listed in the Manhattan telephone book, most of whom advertise in the *New York Times*. Every day hundreds of highly qualified employees flock to their waiting rooms. The interviewers seem to have telepathic powers. They limber up each fresh initiate by addressing him in his Christian name. They advise on how you should present yourself to the new employer. 'Go home and get out of that pullover.' 'Something trim and black. And no woollen stockings, what's more.'

By now I conform to the pattern of the American way of life. After twenty weeks of employment I qualify for relief. Each week a cheque arrives and the postman understandingly slips the envelope under the door. Every seventh day you trip off to the local office and join one of the long queues. Are you able to work? Are you looking? they say. I buy meat wrapped in cellophane that when taken from the oven smells of hot wet bears and tastes of tender nothing. I keep my bread in the Frigidaire. I have given up buying spray to combat the cockroaches that file in batches through the walls from other apartments. At night when someone rhapsodically points to a car dump and a paradise tree outlined against a skyscraper and a smoky purple sky, I heartily join in. I look forward to seeing the old bum sitting on my doorstep when I get home. Like most other people on 14th Street I wave my arms and mutter aloud to an invisible invincible enemy. As any good suburban housewife I enter the subway with my hair screwed into bobby pins and as a conscientious worker I go to bed with a left eye twitch and grind my teeth in my sleep.

Soon the first sign of spring will appear, and what pleasure to sit in the Rainbow Room and watch the temperature rise from 30 to 80 degrees. Central Park will be transformed, with no trace of a bud one day, the next everything will be in bloom. On the busy streets squashed paper wrappings will increase and pretty women appear in their uniform of black with a mink tippet, that can be hired for the evening.

Born Losers

Snow was scuffing down. Snow had settled on coat collars and hats, and had turned to slush on the pavements. Pigeons necked in the puddles. The earth was frosted, and the trees were bleak. Judy hummed as she walked to Maudman. She couldn't remember ever having been so unhappy and contented. She felt rather a fraud going to see Maudman at all. He was experimenting with a new drug that could change people, and not necessarily for the better. Judy was curious. She had tried pot and mescaline.

Grace had hinted that Judy needed to see Maudman. He had performed wonders. Grace wouldn't recommend anyone to him. She had to like someone quite a lot to want to share him.

'If it wasn't for Maudman I'd never have these,' said Grace, and her eyes blazed at her children. She looked as if she could happily have murdered all three of them. The drug was an energizer. Grace was normally very reserved, and had become a compulsive talker since taking it. Judy hoped it would do the same for her.

The two girls had known each other some time. Ferocious debunkers, and ignorant on most subjects, in their opinion nobody was any good, no book, no play. Flattery was regarded with intense animosity. If it came from a man he was a philanderer or a fool, preferably both. Instead of dressing to enhance themselves they played down their pretty figures in what appeared a deliberate attempt to be frumpish. They stumped about in surgical footwear, and attended parties in thick throttling woollens. Up to now both had married and demolished two husbands.

In other respects they differed. For example, Judy had a passion for unstable abdominous babies. Grace chose her men for their looks as well as their instability. Grace created shambles wherever she went; stubs were chucked across a room and left to smoulder on a carpet as if she revelled in being a fire hazard. Grace had better connections. It was through Grace that Judy had got her very last job with Mr Nutt of Nutt Mystic Books. 'I know I con do something with you.' Mr Nutt had said, implying a difficult but rewarding task lay ahead, after Grace had given Judy a tremendous build up. Judy had agreed with him. Judy had trailed out to the Jericho Turnpike and met the Nutt family in their villa on the Expressway.

Five days Judy remained glued to ear phones, typing out taped correspondence. One afternoon she had puzzled forty minutes over Mr Nutt's diligent taped voice spelling out d-i-l-l-e-t-a-n-t-t-i repeat d-i-l-l-e-t-a-n-t-t-i. The sustained abatement of the typewriter caused Mr Nutt to summon her into his office the other side of the glass partition. Mr Nutt never forgave her his mistake. Judy never went back to the Turnpike. Ever since she had been slumped in bed cleaning and counting the residue in her pocket book.

Under the impression she was arriving early Judy lingered over the doorbell. The buzzer responded immediately. A young girl's head protruded. 'Hallo hon'. Forty minutes late. We thought you weren't going to make it.'

Judy entered a stark dungeon reeking of novocaine. An enormous beard dominated the mantle, beside it was a snap of Maudman as a docile cadet under a maternal halo. A large bare desk was covered in dust on which the telephone rested. Framed credentials were stacked on a bench, and clusters of naked wiring sprouted from the walls. Maudman had just branched out on his own after practising at Bellevue the last twenty years.

A big lumbering man, with big booted feet, he had a slight stoop, his moustache bristled, and the intense eyes had a starry wild look. His short-clipped hair shot up perpendicular as if he'd neglected to have it cut recently.

The instant he saw Judy he pulled a hideous face, hitched up his lip and bared his gum.

'Just take a look at my ulcers,' he said.

Jesus! Judy thought. Another hypochondriac just like Daddy!

'It's unlikely we can effect a complete change. All we can do is assess the guilt. Diminish it, and thereby lessen the degree of punishment. I imagine that's why you're here . . . to vary a masochistic pattern.' Maudman regarded his wrist watch. 'This new drug is derived from a fungus. . . . It's been discredited by the medical profession and only gets used in institutions. Don't spread it around you get it here. You may think of me as a genius or an idiot, it makes absolutely no difference to me.' His smile was irresistible.

'Do you ever dislike a person who comes in here?'

'I either take more or less interest. I find the ones who interest me most produce the best results.' He ran a finger along his novocained gum. 'Now let's get down to a few details. When are you going to pay me?'

Maudman noted down Judy's age, the ages of her parents, and their religion which was nil. He wrote down their names, and the names of everyone with whom she had been emotionally connected. He had quite a bit to memorize. In order to complete the picture Judy gave him further information. No breast feeding. Frigid. A bed wetter to this day on occasions. Seduced at fifteen by her father's best friend. Maudman reeled. His laughter sounded like a series of hiccups. 'How did Daddy take that?' was his only comment, as if he and Judy had pulled a fast one.

'He died soon after. I killed him.' 'Wow!' Maudman muttered.

'Drink this.' After taking a sip himself Maudman handed her a glass of colourless liquid. Judy swallowed and waited, stretched out under a blanket in her snow boots. Over her eyes a black mask was placed, the kind a burglar would use. On went the schmaltz. Rachmaninov. Maudman briskly delivered his commonplace:

'Now! You're rejected by your mother the minute you're born. You're a girl. See! A competitor. Also, you're rejected by your father, though he loves you more than this woman . . . your mother . . .

you're his own kith and kin. He loves you more than this woman he's screwing who'd rather be screwed by her father, anyway. Now you want to have first place with Daddy . . . but you can't. Cause this other woman's got him. You're a born loser. Some adapt to this. But your parents didn't handle you right . . . it looks as if somewhere along the line things got fouled up between those two. What it was we don't know. For one thing we're not dealing with your mother, or your father, for that matter, and for another he's dead, anyway . . . so we couldn't if we wanted to . . .' Judy giggled.

'How are you?'

'Fine.'

'Anyway, this makes you all your life one of an out group. We're here to make you one of an in group.'

'I don't want to be.'

'Oh yes you do.' Maudman's tone was firm.

'Can I ask a few questions?'

'Go ahead.'

'What are your interests beside this?'

Maudman paused before stating uncertainly, 'My wife.'

'Besides your wife?'

'Music,' he replied disinterestedly, 'listen to it.'

'Couldn't we have something more modern? Like Wozzeck. What would you rather be doing at this moment?'

'Screwing my wife.' Judy giggled. 'Now,' Maudman was stern. 'Let's get back to Daddy. What can you remember about him?'

'He took me for walks.'

'Well, that's nice, isn't it?'

'It was probably more amusing than going for walks on his own.'

'What did he do?'

'He was totally ineffectual. That's what I hated about him.'

'That's what you think. He didn't screw you. He was screwing this other woman. See!'

'I suppose you have to tell this to everyone. How is it you don't go screwey yourself saying the same thing to everyone every day!'

Maudman's hiccups had a guilty ring, he said, 'These ulcers are killing me. How did Daddy look?'

'His moustache bristled. His eyes were wild, and he stooped. I used to sit on his knee. When I cried he'd hold an egg cup to catch the tears. He knew it would make me laugh. It always did.' Judy had the impression Maudman was asleep. 'Am I boring you?'

The chair scraped as Maudman woke with a start. 'A nice looking fellow. Eh?'

Judy began to writhe. Her stomach distended, and her arms lashed out. Coloured ogres raced through her head and exploded in all directions. They were followed by hundreds of eyes and teeth. Maudman knew the symptoms.

'What do you see?'

'Nothing.'

'Keeping it to yourself. Eh!'

Judy turned into a foetus. She remained for two hours without speaking. Four hours had passed before the mask was whipped off. To Judy it seemed like one. Opposite framed in neon sat Mephistopheles, his goatee reaching to the ground. Judy's skirt was hitched up. She lay helpless and rumpled with a sensation of having done something indecent.

'Don't worry. The ones who interest me micturate. I keep a towel for that event. What is it?'

'You look like a quack to me.' Judy swayed into the bathroom. The mirror reflected two blazing doll's eyes and a pale face unpleasantly bloated. How abysmally shoddy she seemed. No one with pride would be dead looking so down-at-heel. Back in the dungeon, she said, 'What a horrible painting.'

Maudman glanced at his reproduction of the Head of Homer, and nervously caressed his ulcers. 'My wife chose it.'

'Well, you must like it or you wouldn't have it there.'
'We're going to fix you up so you're happy and adjusted like me and Dottie, that's my wife. Dottie's the most important thing in my life. I could give all this up for Dottie and spend the rest of my life in a tent . . .'

Dottie came into the room hoisting a cup of hot water and a tea bag. 'How dee hon'. Time to get you goin'.'

'Sure it's not poisoned,' hissed Judy.

'Wow!' muttered Maudman.

Dottie's hand shook. Her nails were bitten to the moon. The cup rattled, the tea swilled on to the ground as she laid the saucer on a table next to the couch. Judy received a sharp whiff of sweat.

'Dottie and me . . . and me and Dottie . . . and marital bliss,' Maudman crooned. His uxorious eyes probed Dottie's gallant little back zigzagging a retreat. Smiling, Dottie went out giving the door a vicious slam.

'One gets them younger and younger . . . like the child molester I changed once . . . it's a way of getting Mummy before anyone else has had her. This is my third. The first turned into Mummy. The second became a sister. This one's a wife alright! We're going to make you happy and adjusted like me and Dottie. Drop those fantasies. By the way . . . you may walk out of here and fall for the first man you see. It's the effect this business has on people.'

Maudman reeled off the names of famed beauty queens he had changed. He gave intimate details of their compulsions. He said he could have married any one of them. His wild stare returned. With an irresistible smile, he questioned, 'Next week?'

'Tell me, frankly, if you were in my place would you come?'

'You mean if our rôles were reversed?'

'Yes.'

'I'd come to pick the fellow's brains. It takes a real nut to know how to treat 'em.' His eyes blazed. 'Like to pay me?' He edged Judy toward the door. 'Try starving before the next time. That way the potion takes more effect. It's the kind of punishment that should appeal to you. Got somewhere to go? We like to think you're not alone the rest of the evening. Whatever you do don't drive when you leave the building.' His eyes were raving. 'No driving . . .' sounded an incitement. With a violent thumb gesture he hitched up his lip and ran a finger along his gum. 'I hope I'll be able to talk the next time. These ulcers are a bit of a handicap. Two months now. The devils won't quit. Dottie'll see you into a cab.'

From a crouched position Maudman glinted after them up the stairs. Judy had a fleeting vision of a goatee being caught in the door as it closed with a decisive clank. She wondered how many must have terminated a session with a head-on car crash.

Arm-in-arm with bloated faces the two women staggered into the street, neither one knowing who was supporting whom. They thrust through the hooting swirls of traffic. Extricating herself from Dottie's grip Judy hailed a cab. 'Alright now, hon'.'

Judy turned back to watch the brave little wife sway to the kerb, returning ostensibly to aid the next compulsive to some haven of adjusted bliss.

Judy dismissed the cab and strode downtown. How evil everyone looked with their goatees trailing the pavement. She felt ethereal and weightless, and naked from the waist down. Judy was filled with hope. Already, months of despair had lifted. She'd starve two whole days before the next session.

Judy stood on the top step. She could have gone on walking indefinitely. She gave the bell another tug. She had covered seventy blocks and was feeling elated and enraged. Hade Grace decided not to open up! Judy was about to slink off when two enormous challenging green eyes smirked through the window pane. Seconds later a boyish figure in green trousers opened the door a crack.

'I was putting baby to bed.' Grace ran back upstairs to complete a nappie change. In the hall Judy stepped on a blackened banana peel.

In the sittingroom she sat down beside a dirty comb and a plate of cold risotto beneath a large de Kooning.

Grace returned with glasses and champagne. After disparaging their friends, Grace said, 'How's Maud?'

'Talked of nothing but Dottie.'

'Same with me yesterday.'

'Finally, looking at his watch Maud said, now let's get back to you. When are you going to pay me?'

Judy gave a hyena laugh. The girls rocked back and forth shaking with hysterical mirth.

'I said I've spent all my alimony for this month. I'll pay the next if you're lucky. Whereupon Maud thrust an antidote into my mouth one hour before my time was up. He then closed his eyes and dropped off.'

'How do you feel?'

'Nothing except for a splitting head. My stomach's distended as if I'm about to give birth.'

'Resistance! Coming out in physical form.'

'Sure it's not the drug simply?'

'See anything?'

'Eyes and teeth. Whenever money was mentioned, a vagina. Prostitution, Maud deciphered. Then I saw Daddy rushing to attack me. Look into it!, Maud bawled. There was Daddy drained of life like a piece of liver. Fegato Veneziana! Maud was gleeful. Just go on gobbling up Daddy and we might get somewhere. Then I saw Daddy covered in blood. I said, What does the blood mean? Time you were out of here, Maud said, ripping off the mask. He says if anything's going to work, you and I will have to start up sibling rivalry.' Judy glowered at Grace, thinking what a malevolent ring her laugh had. 'What does he think he's getting us into shape for, anyway. With nothing but floating nuts around. Maud agreed. Said he didn't know of a happy marriage, bar his own, of course. The women are all ball crushers, and the men have no balls. Born losers the lot!'

Shaking with cannibalistic cackles they stumped down the stairs to get more champagne from the ice box.

'Hallo,' said Grace's four-year-old, eating an avocado, and rubbing it into her hair. 'Just come from the animalist. Where's Daddy? I'll chop it off when he gets here, if he doesn't get here quick.'

A naked Ophelia with a bare sexy rump and hair flowing over the bannister, she ran upstairs to plant herself in readiness in Daddy's four poster.

It was marvellous the way Grace coped. Judy remembered the time Grace could barely cross the street alone. On hearing of someone's ghastly misfortune Grace would double up laughing. Judy liked her being less heartless. But then Grace had been going to Maudman for years. Grace had lived out every fantasy of cannibalism . . . excretal omnipotence . . . and parental assault, and was thoroughly primed for the right Mr Right. Judy wondered why Grace was still going. Though Maudman had warned Judy any change might not be lasting, in case Judy hoped for too much.

Grace was preparing fillets of flounder. Along the gas ring cockroaches scurried dipping their antennaes in and out of the saucepans.

'I got him out yesterday,' Grace referred to her husband, 'he now only comes every evening to put the children to bed. He refused the good settlement I offered three months ago. I could have had the police in, and got him locked out, but it would have been so dreadful for the children to witness. He doesn't seem to realise I've got all the trumps . . . the house . . . the money . . . how does he think he can bargain with nothing. Maud said, you've married a man not only without balls but no pride. Thought you'd got Daddy . . . stead of which you've an old baby on your hands. Have to break you of that pattern. Watch how he'll immediately start fussing over the garbage. Thinks it'll reinstate him as indispensable.'

A wan handsome man in his fifties bustled into the kitchen carrying four quart bottles of milk. 'These have been on the kerb all day.' He hovered about the trash bins rankly overflowing under the sink. His black eyes on Grace, he said eagerly, 'Like me to vacuum?'

'A maid comes in the morning. Baby's patiently awaiting a nappie, though.'

He gave Grace a pining glimpse and went out.

'He loves you even if he is an old baby. He's a good man.'

'I'll have to marry again soon for the sake of the children. An unattached father haunting the house fosters the illusion they'll get him. Not that I won't find far worse.'

They resumed cackling. Judy could see Grace thought she was angling for an invitation. Judy would have preferred to wake in her own bed, but it was an effort to trek home at this hour.

'Like to stay?' 'Yes,' Judy replied. She was taken up to the attic. The kitchen was left a shambles of broken toys, parings, food plops, stubs and moist nappies.

In the children's room Grace's husband was holding a bottle and had baby on his lap. Showing Judy where she was to sleep, Grace said, 'I've got to be up early. A new nurse is coming. The last left a lingering smell of Harlem about the children's clothes, and preached God all day.'

Judy had a sleepless night. The sheets were stained. The lavatory was blocked. On the floor below baby cried and cried. She heard Grace get up. A scrupulous mother, in contrast to her own, Grace gave in to all the children's whims so as to make them secure.

At eleven nobody was up. Judy made coffee. In the kitchen a new coloured nurse with straightened carrot hair sat reading the comics surrounded by left-overs from the dinner.

Judy went home and got into her bed. Now and then she got up to wash, cook fegato veneziana, count her money and keep the apartment yacht-trim.

Each week Judy starved more before going to Maudman. Passing the shovellers freeing the pavement of snow she felt she was off to communion.

The spring came. Judy was still grooved in cannibalism. She had reached a complete impasse. When Maudman mentioned money she regressed to the womb and lay mutely gasping for breath. After four hours she had to be forced out of the dungeon by Dottie. The only other outcome was the hostility Judy exhibited toward her friends.

Every day Grace rang up and talked for three hours. Judy was always disturbed while cooking or watching commercials.

One morning she was re-heating Daddy when the daily query came, 'Made any progress?'

'Yesterday's session I stayed mute throughout,' Judy replied as politely as she could. 'Finally, Maud said, enjoying yourself? Yes, I admitted. Gotta git you goin' somehow he keeps saying, thumbing through his trousers, as if that'll help. Last night I dreamt he screwed me. That's progress, isn't it?'

'Everyone's noticed a change. You're much less negative,' Grace said, encouragingly, and went on about Maudman's reputation. 'It's growing,' she said. 'He's cramming in women all day. Women are sending their lovers, their husbands, and their children. One entire family of five are going. The Nutts. Remember? Women drop by in the night. Maud hasn't slept in weeks. Since Dottie can't enter a supermarket alone there's nothing but potions in the icebox. Maud'll be having another of his breakdowns soon,' Grace ended on a joyful note, curtailing the conversation to an hour, as she had a new Mr Right she was dining. 'I wonder if you'd care to go to Maud in my stead this evening. I'll pay, of course.'

Thrilled, Judy threw the charred liver away.

The waiting room had been freshly plushed with black tufted sarcophagus couches. Dottie handed round potions and teabags, keeping the conversation flowing with details of Maudman's ineffectualness as a husband.

'Come along. Swallow up,' said Dottie, extending a shaking glass. 'Sweaty little slut. Talking to me like that!' Too livid to speak Judy gulped down the double dose. The door opened and Judy saw a toad's eye suspended on a dirty big toe.

Maudman entered and benignly surveyed his harem. 'Where's Miss Judy hiding?' He needed a respite, and so picked on Judy at the end of the line of hostile women. Judy followed the toad into the dungeon.

'Brought me any money?' Maudman laid down a book and a bundle of newspapers.

'Going to read again all through the session. No wonder we never get anywhere.'

We'd get somewhere if you paid me. Should have had you ten years ago . . .' Maudman sighed. He opened his book and closed his eyes.

'You're looking slimey.'

'Wow!' Maudman started.

Judy lapsed into a foetus. An hour later Maudman woke refreshed. He tiptoed out and slouched round to the butcher.

Back in the dungeon Rachmaninov had got in a groove, and was nagging on the repeat.

'You did it on purpose,' said Judy, 'and the telephone's been peeling its head off.'

'Seen anything?'

'The usual. Eyes and teeth. And a tit.'

'Bite on it,' Maudman said, viciously.

'It's all very well for you to talk.'

'I've been through it. Cost me all I'd got.'

'Another vagina,' screamed Judy.

'Bite . . . I mean look . . .' Judy looked. She was about to sink into an abyss when the telephone rang. She heard Grace cackling. Maudman responded with hiccups.

In bed at the other end Grace was seeking carnal instruction for the new Mr Right. Maudman advised them on each move. 'Hold it,' he exclaimed suddenly, 'Dottie's cooking some chuck. I can smell it.' He rushed out, leaving the receiver off the hook, and continued talking on an extension in another room. His voice reverberated for an hour, passed pleasantly by Judy who kept getting snatches of the conversation. Finally she heard him say, 'Git up out of the sack, you two, and come on in. Bring the family. You can jump the line.'

Maudman returned munching a hamburger bun. 'Should have had you twenty years ago . . .'

'What was that all about?'

'A crockful of shit! Let's get back to you . . . perhaps thirty . . . from the cradle,' he murmured with his mouth full.

'Is there any point in my coming then?'

'I'm not forcing you,' he flared with some of his old enthusiasm. 'After all, it isn't as though you've got Grace's dough. I've a lot on my hands at the moment.' His smile was irresistible.

Two hours later Judy left the dungeon cringing. In the waiting room on the black leather Grace was seated next to a handsome elderly man who had baby on his lap. At the extreme end of the queue was a nurse with carrot hair coping with the other two. When Maudman saw them he turned queasy. Accelerating past, he bolted from the room.

Judy slunk into the night feeling the lowest creature living, not fit to lick the feet of the passing pedestrians. The sun was sinking. The West side was lit in a sultry sulphurous glow. Shuffling toward her Judy saw the biggest toad yet. Every three paces it stopped dead to mutter and rub its gloved flippers together. It paused to give her a second ogle. Judy recognised Mr Nutt of Nutt Mystic Books.

'You've changed,' he ogred.

'I've come from Maudman.'

'Glad to hear it!' He was a little old stocky man in a shabby raincoat. 'Time you found out you're not as good as you think. I gave you the work any high school girl could do. Your output was minus nil . . . Good luck. . . .' His tone implied there was scant possibility of that.

'I'm going through it . . . so is my money . . . no regrets . . .' He shuffled on, stopping dead every three paces and muttering as he fluttered his flippers. Judy watched him turn into Maudman.

Parked alongside the kerb was a horse and wagon with a peddler's licence, and a Bronx number plate. With great verve two healthy tanned men in open shirts were doling out cherries, grapes and watermelons. One could barely articulate. The other resembled a gypsy. His bright pebbley eyes shone with an intuitive awareness of how to instantly profit from a situation. Business was great. They had fallen in good. To remain in such a congested area he had paid off the chief of the neighbourhood police and the two cops on the beat. The residents had complained of being deprived of parking space. Gypsy was moving to a fresh site the following day. Here was this knocked-out broad. The last month every week at this hour she passed in the same red sleeveless dress, with limp black hair and blazing pupils. He'd approached her before and made no headway.

'Hallo Dolly! I've seen you somewheres else.' He took Judy's arm.

'Hallo,' Judy was ravenous. She picked out some fruit. He carried the bag across the street, and helped her on to the pavement. As they zigzagged along, he confessed, 'In all my life this is the first time I've left my wagon in the hands of an affiliate.'

Judy thought him a warm uncomplicated little fellow. He didn't wait to be asked. He followed her into the Brownstone. Before leaving he said, 'You need me. I knew it the moment I clapped eyes on you.'

In a few days Gypsy returned unannounced with a crate. He was shaved. Judy thought he looked smashing in a ripe red sweater and black shoes with a plaid motif. He said, 'I've been thinking of you very heavy.'

'You mean deep?'

'No, heavy. You like cold cuts?' He unpacked the fruit, vodka, sliced cooked beef, gherkins, and cardboard thimbles of mustard. Beside them he laid a horse whip.

Dripping watermelon, the black pips sprinkling the pillow, he said, 'This isn't something passing. I'm hot for you. We're going into business. To think I could have went with you a month back. I'm going to scoop out your liver. Chew you to bits. Rip out your guts till you're dead.' Judy's heart quickened.

He clamped his teeth into her flesh. He rammed down her head. It was all he could do to stop her licking his plaid shoes. Grinding his teeth into her breasts, he said, 'You know one day I'm going to kill you.' As a prelude he bit into a nipple. Judy's scream woke up a neighbour. 'That was delicious,' he sighed at the end, 'like as if I'd brushed against a serpent.'

He sat on the edge of the bed with a box of Band Aid. The brown healthy body had begun to show signs of a pot. Judy felt her aching bruises. He listed his favourite dishes.

'I like my T bone well done, and you? I can't touch fish. The smell turns my stomach.'

At five in the morning he had expounded all the fractional differences of fruit prices in her neighbourhood. It was time to go to market. The bed was searched for the horse whip. The wagon was parked at the kerb, and the horse's head in a nose bag.

'I can see you have eyes for me something awful! I'll soon be back to kill you. I figure like this here, you can lick my feet. Anyways, I'll send some affiliates. They pay good.' Judy ached in anticipation.

Grace telephoned to report on Maudman's breakdown.

'Dottie's gone back to Mummy. Maud's been calling me every day saying he had to see me. I told him to work out his own problems. They carted him away this morning.'

Every day Grace called, anxious to know if Judy suffered bad withdrawal symptoms. Counting the money accumulating in her pocket book Judy always sounded unnaturally cheerful. To the extent, one day Grace remarked, 'You're totally indestructible.'

Judy agreed perhaps this was so.

'Wherever I go I see toads,' she said, and banged down the receiver.

Judy went on counting and waited for Gypsy's penis toes to walk in.

Count on Me

One day in April, to Juliet's delight and surprise, a letter arrived from Peter Dreemer, to say that his wife was planning to join her lover for three months in the summer, and would Juliet care to come then for a 'few weeks sun and swimming'. He, Peter, would love it. Of course he would meet her at the airport. By then he should have finished the novel he was working on, so that being guilt-free, they could do almost anything together, drive through the Pyrenees even—if Juliet hated the flypaper hordes on the French coast in the season as much as he did.

Divorced from her husband, bored and lonely, with no one in particular to interest her, Juliet felt her existence to be vacuous, without point or meaning. It had been the most dismal winter. When not wandering round an exhibition Juliet attended an Art School, or lazed in bed morbidly studying herself in an oval gilt handmirror and gazing out at London rooftops swathed in perpetual grey. In the evenings she prepared neat meals for her girl friends; a scrap soup, fillets of sole cooked in a bought crustacea sauce to which she added cream, and to finish, from Fortnum & Mason, a Cornish cream cheese with oat cakes, the only course she was ever complimented on.

Juliet hardly knew Peter Dreemer, but she had always been intrigued by him. On her honeymoon in Venice some summers back he had been the youngest member of Harry's bar. He had carefully untidy black hair, and was always dressed in white, with very white shoes and socks. Although even then spoken of as having great talent as a new young writer, he looked more like a promising batsman. Juliet had made friends with his wife, Eve. From then, whenever Eve came to England, they would meet.

It was during one of his infrequent visits to London this winter that Peter had seen Juliet again at a party. She had praised one of his short stories from some little magazine, so that Peter had found her appealing. It was then he had decided, the next time his wife left him, that he would turn to Juliet and lean on her. Juliet had never spent any time alone with him, but she was so pleased to have an opportunity to escape from England, that she answered his letter at once, agreeing to join him provided that Eve, whom she knew and liked better, should approve of the plan.

A letter came by return. He was so glad she was coming. He could not give an exact date yet. She wouldn't mention her visit to anyone. He really was longing for it. He remembered their last meeting so clearly. How he was looking forward to seeing her again, and now that she was alone he would like to be the one to spoil her for a bit. In preparation, he was going to have his old car fitted with a new battery, some new tyres and really it could do with a new windscreen. From then on, there was a regular exchange of letters, and instead of moping on the bed Juliet watched for the post. Perhaps as Lord Luck was always predicting, events had taken a turn for the better.

One grey morning in May a postcard arrived with the departure date. If she let him know the time of her arrival, he would of course, be there to meet her. Due to arrive on the first of June, Juliet remained in a happy state of anticipation until the last week of May, when a telegram came to say there would be a delay. How would the fourth of July do? She could come then for as long as she wanted. There was windy and uncertain weather at the moment. The prospect of her coming made him feel so happy and anarchistic. How he longed to see her again, and now that Eve knew and approved there was nothing to stop them meeting. To think of all the magic places they would motor to! He did hope she wouldn't have something better to do by then. She wouldn't disappoint him, would she? She could count on him. He only wished it might be sooner. If she just let him know the time of arrival he would, of course, be there to meet her. Juliet spent the next days going through her address book, as with increasing tension she stared vacuously out of the window and awaited the fresh 'D' date. But all went well. She left London in a rainstorm. At the airport she sent Peter a telegram to say she was on her way. At Nice she stepped joyfully on to the runway and followed the crowd to the Customs. It was hot and a sticky smell of warm cistus greeted her. But there was no sign of Peter Dreemer. An hour passed after the other travellers had departed; Juliet watched several airport buses drive in and away; in despair she focused on the avenue of umbrella pines that bordered the runway and planned, should he turn up now, how she would receive him. Should she be crushing and cool? Certainly, this was not the welcome she had envisaged. Of a sudden Peter came running, in close-fitting fresh laundered white trousers, head down toward her, eager and sunburned, a neatly clipped fringe of black hair sprouting over the V-neck of his tangerine pullover. It was clear he had taken great care thinking up his appearance. With touching warmth and affection he kissed her as though they had known each other a lifetime. How very glamorous she was looking! He'd parked the car in the shade, he said. How happy he was that she'd made it, because HE very nearly hadn't, the alarm had been set for six, but it was only the arrival of her telegram from London that finally got him out of bed. Yesterday was his twenty-ninth birthday. How he hoped that the new decade was going to be as full of delights as the last had been. Thinking of the number of times Eve had deserted him for months at a time during the past years, Juliet turned for some hint of irony, but there was none. Arranging Juliet's case in the back of the car, Peter said that his angelic little wife had been with her lover two days now. This was HER car. HIS was in a garage SMASHED UP. On the night Eve left him, some filthy little estivant had tried to pass on a crossroad, that he, Peter, had collided with a deluge of conifers, and been dragged out unconscious. His hands were covered with grubby strips of Elastoplast as proof of it. Eve was going to be rampageous. Any day now he expected a callous reprimand. The garage reported the repairs would take at least a month, there was no telling what the cost would be. But then think of all the magic places they would motor to, once the car was ready. He was like a God when it came to travelling—if he put his mind to it. But there'd be no fun in taking a trip in this tawdry little vehicle. Juliet was not to worry, just count on him, he always came up trumps, she'd see. Juliet glowed with anticipation as she glanced at his handsome dark head. Jammed between two caravans they joined the double line of cars and slowly drove in a dense procession along the coast, past vast stretches of building lots teeming with holiday campers. Peter talked on about Eve and the novel he was working on. Was Juliet as fastidious as people had warned him? He liked to think it was true. Her visit really was going to be a boon, it would staunch the sense of neglect and loneliness brought on by his wife's absence. How sick he was of the way Eve treated him. He really was going to start anew and make a success of this visit. One couldn't be for ever adolescent. He tittered. Wasn't he getting on for thirty. EEEEh! He studied himself in the mirror. Was he beginning to look just a tiny bit bloated. Never mind. He beamed.

Snake lines of cars extended down every turning. They reached Cannes at dusk. Peter kept to the queue and coasted three times round the croisette before he found space to park in front of the Carlton Hotel. The grey sky was tinged with pink and the sea was choppy, dotted with fleecy ripples; the long masts of the sailing boats swayed to and fro like metronomes. As they walked up to the Carlton terrace they could hear the waves crashing on the sands. Under the striped awning of the terrace most of the painted cane chairs had been abandoned. The hotel flag blew out in sharp gusts and the fronds of the palm trees shook, while in the distance the Esterel shone a dusky blue-black. Peter handed Juliet his pullover.

'Keep warm darling. Order yourself a cocktail. Champagne, anything. I'm going to buy some croissants. How I shall enjoy bringing your breakfast and looking after you here. Sheer bliss.' He patted his lank black hair so that it bunched across his forehead. 'Count on me,' was his final admonition, before breaking into a run and disappearing over the verge of the terrace. Juliet called to the waiter and ordered another champagne cocktail. A group of puce-faced women went by, their heads swathed in bright coloured chiffon; an over-dressed fat one said, 'The boats rockin' ' and collapsed into a chair. Two thin men in canary sweaters briskly walked past abreast, their bare legs blotchy with boil marks; a couple passed, arm-in-arm with marching steps, he clutching, she pleased, her eye roving hopefully round for a new man. Where was Peter? Juliet called for another cocktail. The breeze cooled her cheeks and she wrapped the pullover closer.

'Il fait pas chaud,' said a Frenchman from the next table, looking round for approbation; seeing Juliet he grinned and wriggled. 'Whisky et Gogo,' he repeated, 'hier, J'etais la.' He turned again for her approval. 'Bien, ca va. Whisky et Gogo.' He shouted into the wind. Then louder than ever, 'On s'en va.' The waiter in his white jacket leant over and pushed the glass shutters to, making Juliet feel unwelcome. Where was Peter? He came back swaying a little, without having bought any croissants.

'I thought we might as well stock up on some Novo Brol while we were about it,' he giggled, and held up a bottle. 'Calmant du nervosisme physique et moral. Just the ticket! And here are a few extra bottles of Miltown, Equanil and Sodium Amytal, just in case they are needed. Now just one drink to celebrate.' He went to the bar and ordered a Ricardi. 'One little drink to pull myself together.'

The terrace had emptied and along the croisette most of the cars were on the move. Peter seemed not to notice how disgruntled Juliet had become. He went on prattling about Eve and the novel he was about to finish.

By ten o'clock they had reached his village, twenty miles on from Cannes. The Place d'Ail was filled with tourists. Peter managed to squeeze the car between two plane trees. The suitcases dragged out, he led Juliet by the waist along the thin cobbled streets to his house.

'In season this village makes me feel quite sick,' he said, as they entered a tiny garden surrounded by a high stone wall overshadowed by the neighbours. Peter searched for the key which was hidden in a flowerbed beneath a conifer, blown to an angle of ninety degrees by the mistral. A magnolia cringed alongside, an oleander was in bloom and a vine ran up the kitchen wall, its grape-clusters drooping from the room and shutting out the light from the sitting-room. The house was small and dark and cool. Upstairs were three rooms with divans in them and suspended over the street on a buttress, curtained from the passing stream of holiday gapers, was a newly built-on shower. The roof terrace was exposed on three sides and had a distant view of a lighthouse on a peak with umbrella pines sloping to the sea. Voices rose from the street and mingled with the blare of radios. The rooms were clean and tidy. In her bedroom Peter dropped the suitcase and said, 'You're going to be really happy here. We're doing without a servant. I want to look after you properly.' Later they dined on the vine terrace of the Novelty café on the Place d'Ail, eating a fish stew with vin rosé, and ignored the constant flush and flow of the public lavatory. Peter rationed himself to two glasses of wine. After dinner, Juliet drank an infusion of mint mixed with lime flowers; she saw some people whom she knew, but discouraged them from joining the table. She told Peter he was the only one she wished to be with.

'I'm so glad to have you to myself,' he said. 'The delights I've planned for this visit.'

Back at the house, stretched on the floor on cushions, Juliet lay listening to his chatter. She praised one of his short stories, which Peter read aloud. Only when he had finished his novel would they take a trip through the Pyrenees. Had she been to Basses Alpes? When the lavender fields were in bloom she would find it quite beautiful. He read and talked until dawn, when a rosy glow began to filter between the slats of the shutters; they were still a little shy of each other.

'What's the time?' Juliet asked wearily.

One hand poised on his hip, Peter swayed round the room with a flitcan squirting the corners with neocide.

'Your guess is as good as mine, honey,' he mimicked. Upstairs in her bedroom Peter said, 'What does it feel like to have such an exquisitely pretty little face? I'm going to make you so happy, my darling.' Shaking loose a lock of hair so that it fell across his forehead, he looked over her shoulder into the mirror as he kissed her and smiling said, 'My eyes are my best point, so people tell me.' He kissed her again. 'You kiss so marvellously I'm a little in love already.' The door slammed. Juliet was disappointed to find herself alone at last. She lay awake some time hoping he might return, but it was nine o'clock before Peter knocked on her door, bringing the coffee, just ground by himself, and with it a croissant he'd collected that morning from the kitchen of the Novelty café. Juliet was sleeping. Hadn't they only just gone to bed? But Peter was shaved already. He was wearing a new pair of white twill trousers with white socks and a bright shirt. Juliet thought he was looking charming. Talking, he lay on the bed, crossed his bare feet and chewed a vitamin pill. Handing Juliet the bottle, he said,

'Take one, darling. It'll make your pretty pink nails grow.' Peter reached into his pocket for a Novo Brol and swallowed another pill followed by an Equanil.

'I'm going to reform while you're here. I shall stay in and work. But take the car, my pretty one. Go out and have a nice time.'

Juliet filled a basket with bathing tackle and joined the noisy horde of holiday makers in fancy caps who were shunting and parking on the Place, while the village loafers stood by smiling cynically.

There were plenty of good beaches in the area. The most popular was the Tobago beach in the shade of pines and cistus, with a semi-circular strip of sand covered with tents, and campers preparing meals over smouldering embers. Amongst the rocks, the snorkel breathing tubes of the underwater fishers moved ceaselessly across the surface. Caked in sand and Ambre Solaire, Juliet lay in the sun roasting, an unread book in her hand, vaguely aware of the cooking fumes, tar-congealed seaweed, old newspapers, rusty cans, rinds, crusts and other food scraps, that attracted so many horse flies. When not brooding about Peter, she made sorties into the pale crême-de-menthe water.

Tea-time, when the sea rose, bringing with it the empty flytox tins floating on the surface, was the signal for her to gather her things together and drive back to the village, where she found Peter in the Novelty café, talking to the Provençal waiter.

'Had a lovely time, darling? You look marvellously brown. It suits you.'

'Tu as pris un bong bang?' chimed in the waiter, as he brought her *citron pressé*, balancing his tray in one hand. Juliet went to the house and took a shower. Her room was filled with mimosa that Peter had stuffed into jam jars and arranged in bouquets round the bed. Later she thanked him. With a pleading look he said how desperately he wanted her to be happy.

After that Juliet would often find Peter on a mattress on his terrace, reading scraps of Kerouac, Fitzgerald or Genet. The house was always very clean, with the brooms stacked in the kitchen. Peter never expected any praise, but took his housework for granted; if she volunteered to help he refused to let her do anything. On the days that she was bored with swimming, to the delectation of the overlooking neighbours, they both lay on the terrace reading, Juliet with her bare legs apart and Peter in what he called his 'birthday suit'.

One afternoon he became more amorous than usual. Stroking her thighs he said, 'Who shall I find again as marvellous as you to kiss? I'd like to spend the rest of my life in your mouth. Do you think I can sleep in your bed tonight?' Juliet yearned for him more than ever. The rest of the day her thoughts dwelt on the evening ahead. They sat up later than usual playing Frankie on the gramophone. It was Peter who led the way upstairs. He got into Juliet's bed wearing his jockey shorts and lay caressing her a long while. Juliet responded with ardour. Of a sudden Peter brusquely pushed her to one side, leapt up and fled across the room. At the door he paused a moment to sob, 'One day I'm going to make you really happy, darling. Count on it. You're so good for me.'

Their routine continued as it had been. After swimming, Juliet would stroll back to the house and have a shower, leaving Peter to chat with the waiter. Every so often they drove to Ste Maxime, took a pile of dirty linen, bought the English newspapers and sat silently on the little port reading and eating fresh grilled sardines with slices of lemon, sloshed down with vin rosé. Peter invariably bought himself something to wear. 'You're clothes mad,' she'd tease him, admiring each new purchase, thinking she'd never known anyone so self-indulgent.

In the evenings they would try out some different restaurant. Instantly the proprietor would rush forward to greet them, 'Comment ca va, Monsieur Piero. It's a long time since we see you.' Giving Juliet an odd look. 'Will Monsieur eat his dinner this evening?' With exaggerated attention the waiters would rally round like male nurses keeping an eye on an unpredictable patient. Each dinner was invariably a disappointment, and they seldom went back to the same restaurant, but Juliet always ate a great deal and Peter kept up a monologue, less and less of his dear little wife, but of the novel he hoped to finish and the trip they would take.

What about Spain? Did Juliet know Barcelona? One had to have some knowledge of the language, though. Packages of guide books were ordered from London and Paris, with a Marlborough's self-taught phrase book. Their passports were posted to Marseilles for visas. Now when Juliet returned from the beach, there was Peter in the café studying Spanish with the waiter. 'He's sweet, don't you think?' Many times over Peter would say. 'I've been coming here for as long as I can remember, always behaving rather badly, and the number of times that waiter's picked me from the dust and put me to bed.'

A week passed. Juliet became very sulky. Although from the lunatic way in which Peter sometimes glared at her she sensed he was suffering, she could not stifle her contempt. One evening at the Novelty café, imagining her to be ogling a Frenchman they had talked with on the beach that day, Peter exclaimed, 'Perhaps you'd like me to leave you alone with him, darling?' and left the table. Peevish, Juliet sat on and drank more cognac as she watched the relays of cars being jockeyed into position round the plane trees. She arrived back at the house late. Peter was asleep, still dressed, with his face buried in a charcoal mass of burnt blanket. A tumble of pills were dispersed about the bed. The instant she crept in he awoke. 'I've missed you, darling. What have you been doing all this time?' 'It was boring without you,' said Juliet, 'I won't leave you alone again.' She helped him to wash and undress, and lay on the bed stroking his head. For the first time she felt they were close to each other. Peter inisted that she stay with him for the rest of the night. They remained in bed all the following morning. Peter was leaving to prepare the coffee when he said, 'I knew one day I'd make you happy. It's wonderful not to feel shy any more. From now on everything's going to be bliss.'

A few days later, while happily swimming about the rocks, Juliet collided with a woman whom she recognized from the village. 'What's it like,' said the woman, 'staying with Peter Dreemer? I don't know how you can stand it. . . .' 'Oh, why? He's marvellous about the house, bringing me breakfast in bed. . . .' 'Why doesn't he have a servant? It's not as though he can't afford it?' The woman stretched on her back and frenzedly struck at the surface of the water so that the spray drenched Juliet's hair. 'The last time he got drunk,' she shrieked, 'he broke up his wife's car, I hear. . . .' Juliet moved away and swam back to shore, reaching her small strip of sand as the woman, screeching 'drunk' once more, floundered up the beach to settle a few paces away. Juliet sat on a long while reflectively watching the sea, blue-green in patches, turn to brown, rippling over the rocks in tender splashes. For the first time a cloud appeared and the wind rose, flickering the pages of her book and scattering the dry pine stalks that littered the pretty soiled beach. The temperature grew more oppressive. Juliet put her things together and by the time she reached the village the long spell of fine weather was ended. The clouds had thickened. A thunderstorm was on the way.

At the entrance to the café the waiter stood balancing his tray in one hand.

'Piero,' he giggled, 'est parti.' He had last been seen taking a pile of dirty linen to the laundry. The waiter lifted a glass and made a gesture of bringing up his fist and jerking back his head, as with hunched shoulders, carrying his tray, he lurched round the bar, deliberately colliding into the tables. Even his eyes glazed over. The villagers in the bar laughed with him; some of them got up and did their imitation of a drunk. Led by the waiter with his tray, all the village loafers lunged round the room with zigzagging steps, while the sun-scorched tourists gathered at the bar stools and clinked their glasses for replenishment. Juliet was offered one pernod after another; glumly she accepted. Suddenly, with thunder and lightning, the downpour began; the cane chairs were quickly pulled in and piled against the wine barrels. Water drummed in cascades on the rooftops and swished in a steady torrent down the drainpipes. Juliet thought she saw Peter run across the Place in the rain; she dashed out, but when she reached the spot where the car was usually parked, she found it had vanished. She hung about the café until midnight and went back to the house in despair.

At dawn she was woken by Peter, who reeled in half-dressed and dishevelled. He stretched out beside her on the bed. Petulantly, he said, 'You don't seem very pleased to see me, darling. Perhap's it's because I'm not shaved?'

'What time is it?'

'Your guess is as good as mine, honey.' He looked at his gold wristwatch. 'It says Wednesday. I could have sworn it was Thursday. What were you doing with all those tawdry yokels in the café? You made me feel quite jealous.' He giggled. 'I spent the night with some sailors.' Juliet did not react. Disappointed, he added flatly, 'We're made for each other, don't you think?'

The rain streamed through the open window and formed a pool in one corner. All that day the rain continued. Juliet had to make her own breakfast. Afterwards she lay on the bed and stared miserably at the water streaking across the roof of the house opposite. For the first time everything seemed hopeless. And so it went on for days. The rain falling in buckets. Peter never picked up a broom again. The beds remained unmade; food congealed on the dirty crockery in the kitchen; layers of dust thickened; once the neocide tin was empty, flies multiplied and mosquitos and midges appeared; crumpled newspapers and heaps of black, twisted stubs cluttered the sitting room. There was a Butagaz leakage; fumes seeped up the stairs and settled in the crannies of the bedroom. The tiny garden became littered with the overflow of empties. Convinced that Peter needed her, Juliet chose not to leave. She wasn't going to desert him at this stage. She was certain the day would come when everything would be the same as it was just before the storm broke.

One morning Peter reeled into her room, with a glass in his hand, and stood swaying before the mirror. 'You make me feel quick sick,' he sneered, 'with those tight, greasy little curls. Why don't you go and have your hair done?'

He lay down beside her, the soles of his unwashed feet reflected in the mirror.

'Your pretty mouth's never left for long without its thick coating of red, is it, honey? And I shouldn't think your eyelashes have been exposed to the light since you were born. How I love you, my pretty one.' Soon the room became tainted like a cellar where alcohol had been steadily fermenting for decades. Juliet pushed him away. Straddling a chair, Peter hung down his head and watched a long spiral of spit froth from his mouth, to remain suspended for a long time in space until it reached the tiled floor. Raising his eyes to the mirror, he repeated, 'My eyes are definitely my best point.' He gave a frenzied twist to a clump of hair and with his other arm hugged the chair and swayed from side to side, making a gurgling, retching sound, in a self-conscious effort to disgust her as much as possible.

'It's time I took a Novo Brol. Seen the bottle anywhere? I suppose, you slut, you've hidden it.'

He spotted Juliet's fresh-laundered white pullover which had slipped from its hanger. With a venomous glint Peter leapt up and jumped on it, flicking his dirty, bare feet backwards and forwards, like someone ridding themselves of mud on a doormat, until with an unexpected jerk of the head, in an ecstasy of despair he vomited. Across the room he staggered and stubbed out his cigarette on the bed.

'This evening we're going to have fun,' he said. 'It won't kill us to have one late night, will it?'

Open-mouthed, with gaping trousers, his black hair bedraggled and his face the colour of a blood orange, Peter collapsed on the floor and passed into a state of oblivion. In the early hours of the morning he swayed in to see Juliet before going across the street to a nightclub, to pick up someone with whom to charleston. Back at dawn, Peter passed out again on a mouthful of pills. The awakening was always the same, he'd scoop his tongue and gargle with mouthwash, before setting off to the café, only to return several hours later to black out again, get up and repeat the process. This ritual was kept up for days; the house smelt of rot and corpses.

Juliet was packing her suitcase when he entered one morning. Had she ever seen anything like the ochre-whites of his eyes and his swollen jawline? He really considered he had at last reached rock bottom. It was time to 'pull himself together'. To strengthen this resolution, he drained the dregs of a bottle of pernod.

'Will the rain never stop, my darling? Sorry to behave so badly. The last week I've wanted to be dead. It's ages since I've had that feeling. God!' he groaned, 'how I wish the rain would stop. When the weather changes, that'll be something. Then I shall finish my novel. If I don't finish it soon, then I never will. I really am going to reform. Only you can help me do it. You could be so good for me. It's when challenged I do my best work. My best work when challenged . . .' he repeated, and sighed a deep puff of alcohol.

'Soon we'll set off on our trip. I think I've mastered the language enough to see us through.' He groaned again. 'What's happened to the passports? I suppose now they'll never come. Don't leave me, sweetheart, will you? You're going to stay and look after me, get me well again. I'll make it worth your while, you'll see. . . .' His words drifted out of the window. 'Make me well, darling heart. Cure me. Only you can do it. Because I love you so. Cure . . . Cure . . . Cure me.' He sighed another puff of alcohol. 'One feels so mortally ashamed. I will make it up to you, I promise. You won't leave me, will you? Who shall I find to kiss when you've gone? With you I really feel I want to be unselfish. Did you get me the tisane as you promised? With luck that'll really make me ill. Then I'll get better again. When I'm well I'm going to be terribly good for you. You don't know how much you mean to me. It's caring so much which brings on this desperate feeling. How can you know what it feels to be a flabby fat eunuch.'

'I won't leave you.' Juliet meant it, convinced that she was the one who could help him; his dependency made her care for him more than ever. The next days she nursed him on tisanes until he could eat what she cooked without vomiting. Certain that events had taken a turn for the better, she bought some rubber gloves and did the housework. Juliet now did the shopping; she brought back Toulouse ducks and stuffed them with olives and pimento, or chickens and cooked them with cream and tarragon. Many a domestic evening they spent drinking Vichy. They discussed their trip to Spain and how marvellous it was going to be. A honeymoon. He'd come up trumps, she'd see. He was the one to look after her. Hadn't she put up with so much for so long and adequately proved her love for him? He wouldn't fail her, how could he? Elated Juliet went on with the cleaning. The sun shone and they swam again. Every evening at dusk they went water-skiing. The passports were found at the post office where they had been for weeks, already stamped with the visas. Ready to leave any day now, one evening they decided to celebrate the new resolutions.

'It won't kill us to have one late night, will it?' He would take her to the local nightclub. Juliet very much looked forward to the evening. 'So glamorous you look, my darling,' Peter said, after she had had her hair set in a pageboy. The laundry was collected so that Peter could change into a pink shantung shirt.

In the café before dinner they sipped a little wine, and sat in silence watching the fresh batch of rowdies from Paris flash by in their open tourers. In a restaurant overlooking the sea, Peter lovingly ordered them both a fish soup, steak Bearnaise and wood strawberries. Many times during the meal he rose from the table, saying he must telephone the garage, so that the car would be ready for their trip. What bliss to be leaving this crowded commercial coast! Finally, when he came back he brushed over a dish of pastries; picking each pastry from the floor, with care he dusted it, before replacing it under the plastic lid. After a few mouthfuls of steak Peter impatiently thrust his plate to one side, scattering the sauté potatoes about the spotless tablecloth.

'Something wrong, sir?' the waiter inquired. Over-stressing each word, Peter enunciated. 'C'est tres bon, mais Jé n'ai pas faim, merci.'

Later, standing beneath the amber light above the entrance to the nightclub where the Maltese patron paced, trying to entice passers-by into his cellar, Juliet reluctantly let Peter kiss her. Holding hands, they groped past the bare-footed couples dancing limpet fashion, with their mouths and shins glued together. At a table in the corner next to the juke box Peter ordered her a brandy, for himself a Coca Cola.

'It's a pity you can't even charleston,' he said, and went across to the first pretty girl he could see. Juliet sat alone until the Maltese came over. Would she dance? She accepted. He changed the disc to a tango. When it ended he withdrew his moustache from her cheek and said, 'Excuse me, if I put on another.' A tango was left on the repeat. They steered round the room for a long while. Peter stood against the bar with his back to the dance floor. He came over as Juliet sat down. 'Enjoying yourself, my darling?' She did not reply.

With a sudden crash the upper door of the cellar was flung open and six rollicking middle-aged men tumbled down the stairs; they stripped instantly, revealing brown loose flesh overlapping tiny daisy-print bikinis; the six split into pairs, raised high their legs and capered round the floor.

'Isn't she sweet?' Peter grinned. 'Should I cut in, do you think?' As the leader romped past, shouting for champagne to be brought.

Disturbed by the bedlam, the other dancers fled the floor; bills were paid and the whole place emptied. By the third magnum of champagne the sextet were leaping on and off tables. One of them, an Italian, seized Peter to embrace him. A despairing waiter, rushing past with another bucket of fresh ice, groaned to Juliet, 'C'est horrible, Mademoiselle. Dégoutant.' Peter's pink shirt was ripped off. Would he join them and come to Milan? Juliet, who had resumed her glide with the patron, was soon forgotten.

The sky was a blaze of red as the seven men tottered out to face the daylight. When he reached the top door, still holding his glass of champagne, Peter turned and shouted down, 'Have fun, darling. Remember, it's you I love. One day we're going to be really happy. Count on it.' From a distance she heard his voice drift on with the words, 'Rock bottom . . . reached rock bottom . . .' then a thud and several times the chant of 'my best work when challenged, when challenged', and a final gasp of 'O.U.T. spells out', before Peter fell into the twelve outstretched arms. With rapturous shouts the men carried him shoulder high to the Place. It was the last Juliet saw of him.

During the next days Juliet moped about the house; at night she would head for the nightclub, sit alone with a drink and wait for the Maltese to tango.

A week went by. She used the car to get to the sea and back. Then one morning, sobbing but calm and determined, Juliet put her things together, locked the house and, after burying the key beneath the conifer, she drove slowly along the coast to the airport. Drunk with tears, she booked her passage back to England.

A month later, at a crowded bottle party in London, she was leaning against the bar watching the rock-and-rollers and nursing a glass of port and Martini that someone had rescued from the drink dregs, when across the room, to her delight, she saw Eve's pretty, determined young profile. They exchanged a conniving look and Eve rushed over.

'What have you done with my husband? Why aren't you still looking after him? Don't you know he can't manage alone? There are another two weeks before I'm due back.' She turned for confirmation to her lover, standing staunchly by her side.

'You should never, never have left him. I always thought you'd let him down. Poor Peter. He's so naïve and trusting. What'll happen to him now. Oh dear. . . .' Very upset, Eve hurried from the party, helped by her lover who, glancing back, gave Juliet a swift, killing look.

A Wet Cherry Bomb

The last time I saw Enid she had an ashblonde head, and was a little less muddy looking. Picking her up at her apartment I remarked how shoddy I found New York. Enid glanced scarily round the room to see how it might strike an alien eye.

Outside, lining the street were some huge lumps of manure. She said,

'Perhaps you're right. Three days ago I pointed that horse shit out to Reggie and he said what makes you think it's horse! Reggie'll be at the party.'

As we entered, Enid said, 'There's Jim over there.' She nodded toward a blue silk jacket and white filled shirt hemmed in by satellites. Jim seemed to be half-liking it, at the same time there was a wild plea in his eye for deliverance.

'Where are you staying?' he said to me.

'In a hotel off Broadway.'

'Call you,' he said, kissing me on the cheek, and disappeared with the mob at his heels.

As soon as Reggie Right saw me he got up from his chair. In order to cross the room he had to pass and say something, 'Nice to see you.' he said, increasing his pace. A minute later he had grabbed his hat, and was out of the door. Enid ran after him.

I first met Mr Right at luncheon with Enid. I'd always admired his books, and was thrilled she had arranged the meeting. It was the first really warm day. When we came out of the restaurant the whole of Central Park was in bloom. Mr Right put Enid in a cab, and then walked me to the zoo. We strolled on down Fifth Avenue. In the Rainbow Room two hours we sat drinking frothy pink rum cocktails watching the Newsweek building flash the time and temperature. On the sixth drink, feeling less awed, I said,

'Do you do this often?' and had the courage to look at him. He was

A Wet Cherry Bomb

the dead spit of my grandmother. I was besotted from that moment.

On parting, he said, 'Call you. I'd like to take you down Wall Street one Sunday.'

I looked forward with growing impatience to this lugubrious jaunt. He never called. Two weeks later I wrote a note asking if he'd like to come up and see my drainpipe. He rang immediately and suggested a small dinner that evening. Although that week I'd hardly eaten, I said it would have to be very small. I was on a regime. That seemed to please him.

I arrived late. Sounds of tropical bird life emanated from his apartment. I walked in to a croak of bullfrogs. He was mixing martinis. I felt I should have admired everything, like the highly polished suit of armour, the crossed swords, and the preying mantisses pinned to the walls. But we went on silently drinking. Later, he took me to hear Murphy's Dixieland jazz at the Metropole. The band rose and serenaded Mr Right. Cheered up, he said,

'Like me, you're very withdrawn.'

I stayed the night all the same. He cooked us scrambled eggs for breakfast. 'Another sloppy day,' he announced happily at noon. I was dressing when he said he was driving to Long Island the following day.

'Last night you invited me down. Forgotten or changed your mind.' He looked at me very doubtfully. Did I know it would be a long weekend? There was this national holiday on the Monday.

'Not another! You have national holidays every day of the week here!' He took this for criticism.

'Also,' he said, 'there's this car race on the Sunday.'

I said if he wanted to do anything on his own I was the last person to mind. I liked reading, and could always amuse myself. That didn't go down well. We parted, and he kissed me on the back of the head. He called later and said his temperature was mounting.

'Trying to chicken out! Take buffs. And be at Estelle's at nine.'

'What a pretty name!'

'It's what's known as you can't miss it. Corner of 40th.'

I walk into Estelle's as the car draws up. I ask how he is, and stroke his arm.

'How did you find this place?' he says, pleased with it, but waits in the car.

The drive went well in an old Bentley that one was meant to admire. I couldn't bring myself to, instead I tell him of the woman in the hairdresser who had brown arms and legs and dead white hands and feet plunged into bowls of soapy water.

'She must have got 'em stuck in cement.' His jokes were usually better.

We stopped for more martinis and scrambled eggs. He put his arm round me as we got back in the car. We talked of Enid and Jim. Said last night he'd gone to Jim's farewell. Surmised I'd be there. Five hundred people and who'd paid for it. I said why was it people here never said a party was fun but who paid for it? That Enid had told me Jim had spent all his money on it, and gone to England broke. Though, Jim had a reputation of being so close-fisted he never paid for a thing.

'You kinda call everyone close.' Mr Right said. So we talked of Jim's band leader clothes. 'Gone back with a suitcase stuffed with them, I shouldn't wonder!' And why didn't he go the whole hog while he was about it and get rigged as a matador. Wasn't he effeminate. Poor Enid!

It was sunny when we arrived. The country resembled the outskirts of Dymchurch, only not so pretty. It was a little grey-painted clapboard house with a tiny tower overlooking the bay. He'd described it as remote. There were several others within pacing distance. Anyway, terribly nice, surrounded by wild roses and tall beach grass. Water lapped the front of the house. The opposite bank was bordered by more beach grass the colour of corn. Fat gulls flew over the water. Speckled black birds and swallows fluttered about the porch. I envisaged spending the rest of my life there.

Mr Right donned a Conrad-type yachting cap and mixed martinis.

Several times he changed his clothes. He finally settled for some dashing sick green corduroys and a striped jockey type shirt.

Was I allergic to poison ivy? Also, the undergrowth swarmed with ticks that burrowed under the skin? He said he had a hammering job to do. I changed into purple pants and followed him. A boat with an outboard motor was jacked up in the garage. I had a feeling I ought to commend, but a man arrived with his Bugatti all tuned for the race on Sunday. A long conversation was followed by fierce revving. I fell asleep on the bed beneath a mural of a girl with whiskers that Mr Right said was me.

In the evening we sat on the porch in rocking chairs and watched the boats passing, the birds flying over the dunes, and the light changing. The clouds varied from cumulus to streaks of fleece.

Fibreglass speed boats and yachts passed at the rate of three a minute. The figures on deck gazed shorewards. A faint breeze carried their voices. One would say, 'There's old Righty's house over there.' And another, 'Alright Reg is looped again.' They'd wave. When my hand was not raised in a reciprocative salute there I was wrapped in a blanket carrying cheese spread and bacon thins and dirty dishes backward and forward while Mr Right mixed martinis.

That night we lay necking a long time with me on top clutching the back of his head. 'My beautiful darling,' he kept saying, 'I do love kissing you.' And how he loved my beautiful charlies with freckles on them.

He spent the next morning in the garage tinkering with the Bugatti. Week-enders kept dropping by, bringing one of his books to autograph. Friends called without warning.

After I'd showered and swept he came in with a broken starting handle. 'It won't go,' he said forlornly, and that he'd merely strained himself. Noting the sink, he said, 'So she's cleaned up!' 'Yes,' I said, 'she's cleaned up.'

He got someone to push the car. With a lot of revving and roaring he set off in the Bug leaving me to read in the sun. I followed the sound of the back fire until he must have reached the village when there was a sombre silence.

Two hours later he came back buoyant. 'It's a pretty day. Let's eat.' Once more we drove off, and sat on a bench at a snack cabin. We ate steak rolls and watched the people lined up on a tee, practising golf strokes. One man was so bad each time he hit a boss shot he turned to the eaters for approbation.

'He might as well be using a cricket bat. Do the players have to retrieve their own balls?'

'No, but this one ought to be forced to.' The barman agreed with him. He said he was going to name a sandwich after Reggie.

'An alrighty.' I suggested. Neither of them smiled.

It was much warmer away from the sea. While waiting for the crank to be fixed why didn't we squat in a field. He liked the idea and broke off the main road through a wooded track. We lay in the sun on the grass. 'We kinda hit it off,' he said, bringing out a duster. He soon got bored, tinkered with the tool box and spat on the windscreen.

Next morning we rose early for the race. Taking a book to stave off boredom, a waterproof for warmth stuffed into the dicky with a sun top, a scarf bandaged round my head, and dark goggles I clambered in. We set off with a grinding roar. Mr Right in his yachting cap, and me clinging on to the side, with baking legs from the heat of the engine, every now and then stung in the face by tarry little pebbles rising from the tarmac. Cars stopped. People stared. We arrived late at the track. Mr Right is being announced through a megaphone. I am listed as the crew.

We have a trial run, about four laps. We accelerate going downhill. Racing over the ruts my breasts leap out. With one hand I hang on to the windscreen, the other is adjusting goggles and pinning back hair. I am surprised I don't hate it more. Each time there is a change of gear the car jerks forward hiccuping deafening roars. If kept running too

A Wet Cherry Bomb

long in low gear it burns out altogether. We keep having to have a refill of water. Racing cranks come up and chat. Other old cars roar past. Suddenly, on the fifth lap, for no apparent reason, we lose speed completely. Without a word he draws into the side. We pull out of the race. Mechanics rush up with advice. To my relief we merely get out and make for the members bar. Nothing for it but to watch from the grandstand.

We drink martinis, deafened by the roar. Mr Right miserably mutters something about finding a man to look at his engine, and disappears. I'm already insanely jealous, and keep sneaking looks over my shoulder. I spot his head in a bonnet. 'Can we go soon?'

'If you want to go we'll have to take a train.'

We return to the bar with me bleating on about manners. He turns and talks to a stranger. I walk away. Getting beyond the bar I make for the crowds anticipating a crash round a V bend in the dunes.

Sobbing, I press on. Seated behind a viburnum I watch the turn blinded by tears. 'The last outpost,' he says, an hour later, handing me a puff of his cigar. Peering through the twigs, he says thickly,

'You can be very endearing, you know.'

Back in the bug we sit bolt up in our goggles as if attending a miracle. People come up and push us. Finally, a truck parks in front. We are towed and start up. The last car to leave the track.

The drive home is fresh and pleasant. Jogging along the deserted dunes we do not speak, though his face seems to say, we kinda get along, he remarks, 'Creepy country round here.'

Back in the little house my face is crimson. I have a shower, saying, 'I've taken all the hot water.' It could be taken as a dig as I accused him of using it all the previous evening. We eat outside wrapped in blankets. The rest of the evening, standing alone on the end of the jetty, Mr Right sets light to cherry bomb fireworks and watches them peter out in the water.

Again he shows me round. We stand clasped together in the tower gazing at the moon. I still couldn't bring myself to be laudatory. Downstairs we prepare for bed. He remains by the icebox and goes on mixing martinis. On the fourth he decides to get in. He tenderly picks up my trousers, puts them on a hanger and into the cupboard. 'How bourgeois.' I rasp. This is followed by another attack. I called him a vain mean rotten old lecher. His tongue felt like a serpent's. What's more there was sand in the bed. Why weren't there any books in the house, and why were the floors littered with bobby pins. He stood like a stricken animal. 'I know I'm a slob,' he said, weakly. In bed I say, 'How about a little affection?' In a passionless manner he responded. I said his breath smelt of hot tyres.

Apologetically, he remarked, 'I don't know what's the matter with me,' and fell into a soft snoring sleep.

Next morning he spent in the garage revving the old Bugatti so that the foundations of the little house shook, and me in it in the bed. He came back to shave simply, and get the hell back to the city. He crept into the Bentley shaking, with blood pouring down his cheek. Trying to redeem myself, I say, 'Come on. Give us a quick serpent's kiss,' and offer to put cold cream on the wound.

'I clot easy. I'm alright.' 'Jack,' I wanted to add. 'You putting the boat away?'

'It stays out all summer now.' His tone implied it was unlikely I'd see it again.

Then an endless trek in a rat race of winged automobiles. The only time he brightened was passing the five mile stretch of cemetery leading into Manhattan. 'They must have 'em standing bolt up in there,' he said, and asked what plans I had for any trips. I said most of my zeal had gone. He said he was thinking of having his bedroom made into a workshop and sleeping in the garage, this way he couldn't be expected to have people down, i.e. Me, I imagine. This seemed the final brush off.

He dropped me and my suitcase on the kerb of Park Avenue, a few paces from his apartment.

'We'll have lunch in the park one day,' he said, without noting down my new number. 'You remind me of a girl I once knew called Lady Egghead.'

'That's an insult, isn't it?' He said, 'Yes.'

Weeks went by.

One evening I was having a drink with Enid at the Algonquin. It was drizzling. I felt really low, could barely speak, drank many whiskies, but they had no effect. Enid mentioned Mr Right. Laughing, he'd told her his weekend with me had gone off like a wet cherry bomb.

Wasn't it a brainwave of hers getting us together. She knew he would like me, and I would like him. Made for each other. Wasn't he well-mannered and witty! A very sensitive shy man with more charm than anyone. The perfect escort to a party.

'You're just his type,' she said. 'He has girls like you chasing him from all over the States. He adores women. Quite a libertine.' So far she'd only been in the sack with him once. She'd asked herself down to the country this weekend. Jim was away in Europe. She was looking forward to it and only hoped the weather would change. So saying Enid's muddy head bobbed out into the rain.

The Square

He appeared to be totally bland—a cool cat. At first she was not very taken with him, but there was nobody else to talk to. The few people she knew had moved away. Freshly manicured and shampooed that day she remained in an isolated corner close to the bar. Her escort, a vital superannuated boyscout with a carefully casual hair crop, had been swallowed up by the crowd as they entered an hour before.

It was a large gathering, and although the guests were unaware of it, the party was being given to welcome Mary to New York. The cool cat persistently asked her name. Some celebrities were present. Perhaps this was another one. 'Mary Groom,' she said, finally, and saw his dark face cloud.

Once the cool cat sensed he was not going to get a rebuff he never left Mary's side. Glued to the jukebox they stood listening to the hub in the next room where a jazz band was playing. Aglow with expectancy, new arrivals kept passing by on their way to a dancefloor roped high off the ground like a boxing ring. Couples frenziedly performing the waddle and the mashed potato looked about to hurtle into the chattering guests below. The cat led Mary to the dancefloor. He was lithe and garrulous to dance with, and wore no underpants. After a brief and abortive attempt to get Mary going in a waddle he resignedly gave up. They adjourned to the jukebox.

The cat slipped some coins in the machine and studiously made a choice. He said it was square to like Ray Charles, he was too commercial. Miles Davis was the only serious jazz player. Miles played for himself, not to please an audience, in fact the last thing he wanted to do was to please. Miles was suspicious of white people and treated them like nothing, often walking out of a place if whites came in while he was playing. There was nothing square about Miles. He was a friend of Miles, Mary could meet him anytime. Also, he was a friend of Jimmy

Baldwin, Ken Tynan, Sugar Ray and Harry Belafonte. There was nothing square about any of them. Mary could meet any one of them. Mary, apparently, was very square, he repeated with manic vehemence, carried away by her silent receptivity. After several more visits to the bar his tone became increasingly derisive. The fact that Mary accepted him without reservation merely made him contemptuous, and the initial sycophancy vanished. Everything she did or said was square, the cat stressed, languidly poised beside the jukebox, his white cuspids gleaming behind the grin that revealed the gold in his molars. He pinpointed various features. Those cultured pearls, for instance. The stark blue print. The shoes. Didn't she know rounded toes were in? His eyes settled with blazing mockery on her hair. Why so long? Everyone was wearing it up these days. Had she been born yesterday? His manner bordered on insolence with a hint of desperado.

Grateful as she was to have been paid some attention Mary was not altogether displeased to see her escort's head bob alongside. Superannuated boyscout had covered both rooms thoroughly, twisted twice, rather well Mary noted, and feeling there was nothing further to be elicited from this pack he now expressed a desire to press on to the next party. Mary introduced him to the cool cat. They did not hit it off. With a glare of approval at her legs, the word square still lingering about his lips, the cat slipped a card into Mary's hand.

'Andiamo,' said SBS, with a raucous party bellow, and 'Ciao,' to everyone they passed on the way out. In the cab peering down at the card Mary read, Ham Burger the 2nd. Promoter. Harlem.

Mary never discovered how Ham Burger traced her, but the next day he announced himself on the telephone. 'I nearly regurgitated when I got back last night.' He sounded apologetic. He happened to be in the vicinity, he added, just passing her hotel, in fact, in Jackie Robinson's Jag. Would she care for a spin? Mary was polite but evasive. Was this the incentive he needed? From then on Ham was seldom off the telephone. A part of her was curious as well as exasperated by the persistence which she interpreted as pushing and insensitive. Her tone was encouraging, though, so he went on calling.

One hot afternoon Ham called to say he happened to be just round the corner in a Bird. Also, he had a folio of Thelonious Monk records to give her. This was tempting. Mary agreed to meet right away, only allowing time to reach Patty's bar next to the hotel.

The crowded bar was lit by pink bulbs and everyone sat about in a haze of tobacco. Thinking she saw someone she knew Mary panicked and fled. Back in the hotel she never answered the repeated peals of the telephone.

Ham Burger called next day, 'You were late,' Mary said, 'I don't like waiting in bars.'

'Square, aren't you!' came the pat response. Ham went on calling. Mary was embarrassed. She imagined the girl on the switchboard was listening in to their conversations.

One hot July Sunday Mary was alone with nothing to do. Although she lived on a family allowance and had no money worries, she was seeking work with a press agent. Nothing had materialized and her morale was low.

Sunday can be a lonely day for someone new in a city. Every minute can seem a masochistic vacuum. From the street the clopping heels of the church-goers could be heard on their way to a service. Car doors were being slammed with purpose by those off to a beach zone. The telephone was a welcome intrusion.

Ham was back from Kennedy airport in Sugar Ray's Mercedes. He had just seen him off to Europe, and now happened to be right round the corner. What about a spin? Jones beach was on Mary's mind. She agreed to meet.

An hour later she walked out of the hotel. For a moment she could not be certain it was the same man who had been calling so unflaggingly the past weeks now standing on the kerb beside a white convertible. She paused, waiting for him to approach. There was nothing distinctive about him, that was it, apart from the way he was dressed stylishly in white with white shoes and socks in contrast to Mary all in black, and the fact he was a negro. A chauffeur with a red carnation sat at the wheel of the car. Squeezed in between the two men, Mary was very aware of the bellhop's interest.

It was a sweltering day. Mary even wore black stockings and a girdle, in order to appear formal, she thought, and not give any encouragement. They drove through Central Park towards Harlem.

'They say the black people are going to rule the world.' Ham laughed. 'Have you heard the story of the little black boy in the Catskills who found some white paint in his back yard?'

'No,' Mary glared.

'Well, this little black boy found some white paint in his back yard and was painting his face with it when his Mammy came out and caught him. "What are you paintin' yor face for like that . . ." she said. "Cos I want to be white," said the boy. "Just you stop paintin' yor face or you'll get a good beating," said his mother. But the boy went on painting his face. So his parents took the paint away. "There you are," said the boy, "I only bin white five minutes an' already I'm hatin' two black folk." ' Everyone laughed. The chauffeur remarked:

'You brought the house down with that one, Bud.' Mary turned to face the windscreen and watched the mounted police galloping through the park.

'Hey listen!' Ham scrutinized her pale plump mug with doubt and interest. 'Did you bring your swimsuit? Cos we're going swimming.'

Mary brightened. 'Jones beach?'

'We're visiting some friends of mine in Connecticut.'

'I have to be back by four,' she lied, gazing into his shrewd brown peepers.

'How's that! I had a feeling you were going to hang out tonite.' The chaffeur laughed with him. The car stopped in the quad of a large new apartment block in the centre of Harlem. With a relaxed sway of the shoulders Ham moved stealthily across the tarmac, the balls of his feet lightly touching the ground as if to test it for safety. The clipped woolly head vanished through the swing door. The chauffeur hurried Mary to an open sportscar parked in front. He slammed her in calling, 'See yer,' and drove off with a manic wave of the hand. Ham emerged with a tennis racket.

'Why didn't you come in this car in the first place?'

'It was being cleaned. See! Suppose I'd arrived late. You'd have stood me up again. Right!' Congregations were streaming out of the churches on to the wide tree-lined avenues of Harlem. Women with high wigs set in the latest Jacky fashion were dressed in their best, in starched blue and pink organdie, in satin, and in tight black lace with flowered hats. All wore cotton gloves. In the churches the raised voices of the preachers could still be heard joyously intoning, Holiness becometh thy house, Lord. Amen. Those who remained in the pews joined in with a chorus of Yes man. Amen. Jesus saved us. Right folks? Yes man, chimed in the churchgoers. Jesus saved us. Yes man. Amen.

On 135th street men in bright shirts stood chatting in a doorway or squatted against a wall outside a crowded bar where southern roast chicken and chips were being bought in cartons to take away. Those set on a date strode purposefully past in brown-and-white co-respondent shoes and tight café-au-lait silk suits, their bootblack hair slicked and straightened. Open trucks loaded with water melons were parked on the side streets. Pedestrians were buying slices of fruit and spitting the black pips on to the pavement. In the public gardens a week's heavy rainfall had freshened the trees. The paths were scented with elder blossom. The grass was lush and green. Men lay sprawled round the boles of the Paradise trees awaiting to participate in a lethargic game of baseball. Some lolled on the benches, protected from the sun by straw hats with white check braid. Others threw dice along the gravel and gambled with dollar notes in their hands. The elderly sat engrossed and bent over a checker board. In the playgrounds the temperature was eighty-five in the shade. Bare to the waist the basketball players had white kerchiefs tied to their brows to stave the sweat. Children were amusing themselves with cardboard jet planes, as their mothers perambulated. In the dim back streets where even during the day strangers feared to stroll, the desperate lay slumped against the trash bins, the gutters were filled with empty beer cans, squashed wrappings, fruit parings, cigarette and icecream cartons.

Ham stopped twice on the way to the country, each time drawing into the grounds of a white clapboard house and parking behind a convertible close to a swimming pool. An immaculate owner greeted them. He then vanished to put on the latest jazz tape. A formal introduction followed. 'Bob Kennedy the second' or 'Meet Billy Roosevelt.'

Rum with iced tea spiced with mint and lemon appeared. There was no conversation. Everyone sat silently round the pool as they sipped their drinks and listened to the throb of Thelonious Monk's Blue Note or the Mitchell Ruff trio.

His legs sprawled out langorously in Brooks Brothers pants, a wrist held limply over the glass as his long fingers toyed with the stem, in mocking appraisal Ham would catch Mary's eye, as much as to say, 'What do you make of us? Civilized. Eh!' Then the host walked them to the car, said 'See yer', and waved them out of the drive.

Finally they pulled up behind four cars in a drive surrounded by meadow-land ablaze with wild flowers. Strapped into orange life jackets little girls with white bows pinned to their plaited pigtails were clambering in and out of a pool. Parents were squatting round with their legs dangling over the edge. The sun had reached its summit.

'Can I lend you a swimsuit?' said a scrubbed commanding hostess.

'No, thank you.'

'Hey! Take off your stockings, at any rate.' Ham's gaze returned to Mary's legs as if seeking some deformity. Hotter than ever, and aware of everyone's interest, Mary walked self-consciously up the stairs. In one of the bathrooms she took a shower. The hostess brought two monogrammed towels. Mary shed her stockings and girdle and settled in a chaise-longue in the garden. Under an awning a foot away Ham lay indolently back smoking a cigar. They remained eyeing each other in silence.

'I've had quite a night of it.' His lids clamped down and he dozed. One hour later his brown peepers were open. 'Hey! How you doing? You'll be the same complexion as me if you sit in that sun. Why don't you take off your clothes. It makes me hot just looking at you. How would you like to hang out with someone like me! Too square, aren't you?' He laughed, surveying her hard, anticipating a reaction. Nobody came over and talked to them. They might have been invisible. Mary remarked on it.

'If it's a man you want you'll be disappointed. They think you're my woman . . . yes,' he reflected, as if titivated by the idea, 'they think you're my woman.' Laughing, he moved across to the pool and dipped a toe in. Shuddering, he withdrew his foot, and bending over bantered with the children, joking about his cowardice. Every so often he glanced in Mary's direction. She heard him say:

'Go over and talk to her. She doesn't bite yet.'

'Is Ham married?' Mary asked the man who sat beside her.

'Ham's looking for some outside activity.'

'Does he have a girl friend?'

'Oh! He's not settled there. But you're all right, you two. You seem to communicate.' There was silence but for the children splashing in and out of the pool. 'Yes man!' said the friend. 'One day the niggers are going to get the power in this country. We're going to change the power structure. Yes man! We won't accomplish anything until we do. . . .'

'Yeah!' Ham said, 'We're big and black and strong. All the black men should get together and get the rich white women. The Vanderbilts the Rockerfellers, get their women fuck them real good and take their money. Take the women from those mother fuckers . . . free them

from those bitches. The white men aren't screwing them anyway....'
He laughed. 'We smell bad ... we steal ... we're feckless and limited intellectually ... but shit man we can fuck those white women real good.'

'Then you become like the white man ... become like the white man and lose your soul.' The friend got up and walked away.

They were asked to stay to dinner. One or two Mommas appeared from the rear. The table under the awning was laid with a bottle of French wine to drink with the spare ribs and bindis. Ham kept peering over his glass with a quizzing look.

'I expect you thought you were going to be given chitterlings and water melon, that we'd eat it in our pinkies and spit the pips in the pool,' he roared.

As they drove back to the city, Mary said, 'How long have you lived in Harlem?'

'Three years.'

'Where were you before that?'

'My grandfather was Governor of South Carolina,' he said with satisfaction.

'What did you do when you first came to New York?'

'Got myself kept by a white woman,' he laughed. 'Now you've got a big black man from Harlem I'm going to straighten out your sex life. You wouldn't want anyone to know you hang out with a black man, would you!' he went on laughing until he reached his apartment building.

He was going to take Mary to a nightclub. Once Ham made up his mind he wanted something he was most coercive. With childish persistence he went on demanding until he attained his goal. Some fear or caution prompted Mary to withhold an immediate acceptance, but she had come to a decision from the outset. Mary had never ventured into Harlem. Even Small's Paradise was out of bounds to her friends who had been warned of the violence. How women were mugged in the street and cabmen beaten up and robbed by heroin addicts. Coloured workers were still excluded from jobs other than manual labour on the new Government buildings going up, and the picketing of shops had increased. It was considered daring to cross Central Park after dark. Some cab drivers refused even to go so far uptown. With Ham it would be different. Mary felt very swinging.

Going up in the elevator Ham said, 'It'll take me five minutes to change.' As soon as he entered his apartment he put on a jazz tape. The rooms were simply furnished. The covers had a plain design, and the walls were white. The shelves were filled with records. There was a view of the Triboro bridge from the terrace. Ham poured himself a whisky. Mary refused a drink.

For the second time that day Ham brushed his teeth, shaved and took a shower. Then he sprayed his body with Arome. Stripped to the waist he kept going in to change a record until Mary became impatient.

'Don't you know. I'm trying to excite you,' he said.

Ham had never been able to bring himself to make love to a white girl as his friends did. One night it was all fixed for him to have a dancer they'd brought back from the Village Gate. At the last minute Ham backed out. He felt he wasn't quite ready for it. 'That's how the whites have beaten me down,' he joked afterwards to his cronies. Mary's docile manner dispelled some of his timidity, but afraid of being rebuked he repressed a desire to kiss her.

A television screen was set beside the unmade double bed. The sheets were rumpled. On the floor a frilled bathcap and some rollers lay next to a book on How to Get Rich Quick. As Mary powdered her face in the mirror she suffered a twinge of jealousy.

First Ham took her to the Apollo. The star turn was a comedienne, Moms Mabley, whose jokes were mostly political with references to the coloured curtain. The master of ceremonies kept mopping his brow with the words Wait till I've wiped my bald, folks. He received wild applause from the packed audience, many of whom were standing at the back of the jammed music hall. There were four girls in tight white satin who sang 'Momma didn't like' to the accompaniment of an electric organ. A strip tease whose hips twitched as she danced as if attached to a vibrator.

They took a cab on to 125th street. Young and old were jiggling in time to Small's band. Outside a crowd had gathered to gape at the couples waddling on the pavement.

Mary was the only white girl at the crammed horseshoe bar lit by iridescent stars flickering on the ceiling. Ham didn't jig. Now that he had given up being a bookie for the numbers, an illegal gambling game, and was a respected property owner he considered it beneath his dignity. Once a week, smoking a Havana, Ham drove round Harlem collecting the rents from his tenants. He claimed that due to rent control he was broke, but he always had money to spend.

Before walking off to the Men's room he glanced along the bar at the row of faces and laughing said, 'Don't go. Cos you can't replace me.'

They crossed the street to Count Basie's. Men were drooped over beer glasses with their heads nodding to the rhythm of an electric guitar. They stood drinking whisky at the bar. Ham tentatively put an arm round Mary's waist and she did not push his hand away.

It was late when they dropped into the Red Rooster. 'Just for connections,' Ham said, 'I do some of my best deals here.' He held her hand as they tottered down the steps into the busy interior.

Everyone in Harlem grew marijuana in their windowboxes so Mary had been told. Thinking she was being swinging, she said, 'Can one of your friends get some pot?'

Ham was shocked. 'Shush! Do you want to get me arrested?' He hurried her out. He told the cabman to drop him off just inside the park, and handed Mary five dollars. 'This should cover your fare. You might even make on it!'

'You're not going to see me home?'

'It's late for me to cross the park. Don't be cross. If we part like this I won't feel comfortable.' He slammed the cab door shut. Mary felt let down. Days passed and Ham's calls seemed to have ceased. But a week later they recommenced. Nothing much was said. It was like a doctor's check-up. 'How you doing?' or 'Been productive lately?' Sometimes he suggested meeting for dinner. It was always a last-minute invitation, and Ham always brought along a friend. The three would sit in Birdland, the Five Spots or the Village Vanguard and listen to jazz. One time when Mary was accompanied back to the hotel, and they took her to the elevator, the woman at the desk bawled across the lounge, 'Now then, you lot, none of that.' Desultory characters sitting embedded in newspapers looked up startled, and stared without averting their eyes until the two negroes had left.

Mary got over the embarrassment of being seen with two coloured gentlemen. In fact she derived pleasure from going to bars and restaurants with Ham always so strikingly groomed in his Palm Beach suits and shirts. She had a better time with Ham than with other escorts who often gave the impression they could barely meet the check. Mary was proud to prove she lacked any race prejudice. She saw herself as a do-gooder. It was gratifying to think Ham was proud to be seen with her. She studied the race question. In a reputable magazine she read the only solution to the race problem was increased miscegenation. That so long as a white face encountered a black the guilt-hate would persist.

Determined to do her bit Mary would introduce Ham to her friends, limbering them up beforehand by saying. 'He's as black as your hat, you know.' He was labelled Mary's blackie. Everyone got on well with Ham who always settled the check before anyone had a chance to look at it.

It was Ham who was ill at ease. Beneath the sick jokes lurked a desperate paranoia. He knew that as soon as he was seen with a white girl it was assumed their relation was sexual. His pride was involved. He did not relish being regarded solely as a sex symbol. Also, he feared the stares of disapproval.

It was the end of August. The sky was overcast. It had been ceaselessly raining for days. The atmosphere was clammy, and it was almost too hot to move. Patty's bar was already lit, its sign swinging hazily over the rain-soaked street. The traffic made a swishing sound, and the headlights of the cars were turned on although not yet six in the evening.

Ham's tyres splashed to the kerb of Patty's. Round the corner Mary had rented a furnished apartment while Ham was out of town on a business trip. He hadn't been home for a week. Ham had spent the afternoon frittering in bars all over the city, celebrating his return. He ordered another whisky and went into a telephone booth. The hotel gave him Mary's new number. Her soft prissy voice was welcoming.

'Where have you been all week. I'd given you up,' she said.

'Are you alone?'

'I've just stepped out of the shower.'

'Step back in then,' he laughed, 'I'll join you. I happen to be in your vicinity.'

The door bell ran ten minutes later. Mary hadn't time to switch the lamps on. An Art Blakey record was playing. She was surprised to see him alone for once. Ham swaggered to the drink tray and poured himself a whisky. He laid his jacket on a chair. A cigar between his teeth, he slipped the chain of the door across to prevent anyone from entering. Seeing a man's shirt hanging on a hook in the bathroom, he cried, 'Hey! You've had a man up here. You've got a beating coming.' He grabbed at Mary's flowered housecoat. 'What you got on under there. Come on, white woman, let's have a look at you.'

The grip on her arm tightened. Frightened, Mary held back. She was hauled across the room resisting all the way with her feet dragging the bare boards. One foot got caught in a table leg. Together they fell rolling over a piebald rug. As soon as Mary rose to her feet she was pushed against the wall. A picture clattered to the ground, but neither were aware of the sound of broken glass. The more she resisted the more excited Ham became. He dragged her back across the room buffeting the furniture as they went. She was flung on to the couch. He ripped off the housecoat and stood looking down at her naked, the skin bruised and lacerated with streaks of blood on the thigh. Her feet lunged out. Ham struck her across the head. Mary gave up struggling. Her head throbbed. Powerless she lay leadenly imprisoned by his weight, clasping his woolly head to prevent herself from falling again.

There was silence in the room. Rain spattered the windowsills. Suddenly both were roused by a scream. Mary had been dreaming. Beetles were crawling over her. Large fat beetles were on the walls, on the couch, and were crawling over her face. They were in her ears and scurrying through her hair. She couldn't shake them off. A sensation of cold slime swept over her.

She broke out of the nightmare as Ham reached down and slowly tied up his shoelaces. He felt ashamed, dazed and panicky. He was playing it cool again. Mary's hand rose to her aching teeth. She raised a pleading face to his. Sheepishly Ham said, 'Square, aren't you!' and picked up his jacket. He walked coolly across the room adjusting his tie as he went, and unlatched the chain. The front door slammed. All that remained of him was a half-smoked cigar in the ashtray. Outside in the street a rapacious blustery wind blew. The rain struck his face. Ham quickened his steps as the thunder broke overhead. White devils were out to get him. Fleeing he hurried along the street. He should have been home at six.

Back in the sanctuary of Harlem he tiptoed into his apartment. He undressed in the hall and crept into the bedroom. His hand groped toward his wife asleep beside him. He felt for her breasts. Waking she said, 'I was worried about you. Where have you been all evening?' Ham didn't answer. He moved closer and embraced her, and at dawn fell asleep feeling soothed and liberated.

Dorothy, Get Yourself Analysed

A keeper in a grey uniform stood with his back to the wall, he was hosing the elephants, aiming at their dry, wrinkled flanks flaked in sawdust; they were big Indian elephants, a male, a female and a baby, with small ears and uplifted trunks, and each had a smile on its face. Water jetted through the tusks and with high-pitched whinnies of delight each elephant coyly shifted its gaint to benefit from the flow. The keeper went on thoroughly hosing, every time he stopped there were whinnies for more. He swilled out the yard and methodically hauled in the piping, then the keeper passed on to the next cage. The elephants lowered on to their flanks and lay wallowing in the muddy whirlpools that had formed in the yard.

It was the first day of spring and the temperature was sixty degrees; there was a cool breeze, but the sun was warming up. It was a perfect day for the zoo. A woman stood at the rails, she was wearing black sandals and her grey hair flopped to a black turtle neck pullover; she smiled as she watched the elephants. In repose her mouth was drawn down at the corners and gave an effect of toothlessness; aware of this, she sometimes sustained a deathly fixed grin. The hosing was over and the woman moved on to the rocky pool for the seals. The seals were being fed, and their webbed paws reached up the keeper's leg, they padded after him to the exit and the keeper stroked their sleek heads, then he turned and ducked under the stone ledge.

'Where are the small mammals?' the woman asked.

'They're scattered. You'll find some over there,' and he pointed into some bushes, 'and some over there.' He pointed in the direction of the Lion House.

'Thank you,' she said, and walked on past a rhino. The woman rounded a bend. There they were, just what she was seeking, a whole colony lay sprawled in the sun; their black muzzles were raised heavenward and revealed the sharp white fangs; they were clearly sated with eating, and apple rinds cluttered the stone paving. It's strange they don't have any trees to climb, the woman thought, and called, 'Minny, Minny, Minny.' One of the animals stirred. 'Minny, Minny, Minny,' another twitched in its sleep. A few people stopped at the rails to look. 'Minny, Minny, Minny,' but none of the honeybears moved, their paws were drooped in the sun and their snouts suspended upwards. Someone threw a handful of peanuts.

'They eat fruit,' the woman said, 'preferably peaches and muscats. They're affectionate little creatures.'

A stranger laughed and said, 'They look as though they can bite, too.'

'Minny, Minny, Minny . . .,' the woman called. One of the bushy little creatures yawned, stretched its legs and waddled slowly forward. The woman bent down and eased her wrist through the bars, the animal thrust its head forward, she stroked the down of the pelt and a small black tongue shot out and licked her hand all over. The woman remained some time amusing herself in this way. People came and went. Immersed in thought, her mouth drawn at the edges, finally she walked toward the exit. On her way out of the zoo the woman bought a frankfurter tasting of varnish, and drank it down with Seven Up. She walked out of the zoo to a bus stop.

'Poor little Minny,' she said aloud, and went to the rear of the bus as tears were running down her face.

*

The Minns used to live far from any neighbours in an isolated farmhouse in the country. They were a childless couple, they loved each other, and they squabbled all the time. Dorothy Minn loved the old house, it was small and oak-beamed, and had once been a cowshed; the rooms were distempered in flaming colours symbolic of love, crimsons, reds and pinks, and the doors were painted white, so that the overall impression was of a Neapolitan ice. There were bright chintz covers, open brick fireplaces with huge logs piled on either side, and bellows and brass firedogs. The dormer windows of the tiny upstairs bedrooms were a landmark for miles around, standing out from across the valley like watchful hooded blinkers. The glazed brick face of the house had a trellis of ramblers and there was an assiduously tended garden back and front. The Minns loved the garden, though neither could boast of having a green finger. The lawns received regular doses of weed killer, made evident by an occasional brown patch, proof of someone having been a trifle heavy-handed. The garden was cut off by a bramble hedge from the surrounding fields where Guernsey cows roamed and lethargically chewed the cud.

Minn was kind and gentle and broody; he was a landscape painter and had quite a reputation in London, where he gave an exhibition every other year round Christmas. While Minn painted in the attic converted into a studio, with nothing in it but a divan and an easel, in the kitchen his wife was concocting some gourmet dish, Oysters Bordelaise, Coq au vin and Poule Supreme. When not plunging live lobsters into boiling water, scraping a pan or skinning a rabbit freshly snared in the garden, Dorothy stood at the kitchen window gazing at an outdoor privy smothered in jasmin. During the summer the sickly fragrance of the yellow blossoms wafted through the house.

Many pretty plants flourished round the privy: honeysuckle and wistaria and flowering quince with pink confetti-like petals, cistus shrubs with their sticky, odorous leaves, and all manner of herbs abounded: basil, tarragon, fennel, sage and a baytree. Next to the privy was an arbutus where nine guinea-fowl went to roost at dusk every evening. On the grass, in the shade of a walnut tree, was a wrought-iron table ready for a delectable meal.

Minn suffered from moods of gloom; he would lie daydreaming for hours in a steaming bath, groaning and humming, 'Oh! To be a million miles away. A million miles from here.'

Dorothy was a fanatical cleaner; she just couldn't stop herself cleaning and polishing the furniture several times over every day. 'You're tiring yourself out, Dorothy. Let me help you,' Minn would say on the stairs as she passed with a broom. 'I can't bear to see you doing housework,' Dorothy answered.

One day Minn remarked, 'Our lives are made intolerable here with no servant. Yesterday I stopped off at Bessie's. She's dropping by this afternoon for an interview.' Dorothy agreed it was a good idea.

Bessie always wore Wellingtons, a green beret and spectacles, and her old face glowed with belligerence. It was fifty years since Bessie was jilted; she had remained a spinster living in a caravan in a field close to the Minns. If Dorothy were in the garden and Bessie passed, followed by a decrepit black spaniel, she smiled as Bessie went by, and sometimes Bessie glared back. Apart from an occasional tradesvan, Bessie and the hunt were all there was to be seen in that remote area.

'I used to know this darned old barn in its cowshed days,' Bessie said, stomping after them up the narrow stairs. In the bedroom she muttered to herself aloud, 'Bloody dark in here.' Bessie was leaving by the back door when the butcher appeared in a white apron stained with offal; he was carrying a tray with two trotters. Seeing Bessie, he whistled.

'Good morning, Bessie. Doing an honest day's work for a change?'

'Pigs or calf?' said Bessie, 'if they're pigs I can't eat 'em.' Minn walked her to the gate.

'Would you like to work for us, Bessie?'

'Are you two married? I'm a churchgoer,' said Bessie, glaring at Minn. Some Sundays the distant chimes of the Gothic church were heard from across the meadows. The intermittent services were attended by about twenty disconsolate parishioners that did not include the Minns, who merely used the neglected, overgrown graveyard with its yew tree dating from William the Conqueror as an objective for their infrequent strolls.

'Mrs Minn would like you to help us out.'

'What's more she ain't bad looking. But why no children?' Bessie tottered through the gate. Minn was back in the house when Dorothy said,

'Bessie seems quite a character. But she makes me feel I'm not very nice to know.'

It was after Bessie had been coming a few times that Dorothy's mania for cleanliness grew worse. As soon as Bessie arrived in the morning, loud crashes could be heard in the kitchen. Each time Bessie left, the Minns checked to see what plates were missing. The waste bucket was scoured for chips, but all they ever found was Minn's gold cuff-links thrown out on the compost heap. 'She's so blind,' Dorothy wailed, scrubbing the kitchen floor, although Bessie had just been over it.

'I'm so sick to death of seeing nothing but crows and sheep from the window. And those damned gulls that fly in from the sea portending more bad weather.' Minn felt one of his moods coming on. To stall it, Dorothy said,

'Let's get out of this hell hole,' and she meant it. Next day the Minns went to London.

During the bleak winter that followed they began to pay regular visits to the city. On a cold, frosty morning as the sun rose out of a meadow haze, a taxi crept into the drive to take them to the station. The routine was always the same. The chaffeur would hoot at the turn in the lane and Dorothy would call, 'Hurry up, Minn.' 'Stop nagging.' 'If I didn't we wouldn't make it.' The Minns were the last to board the early commuting train, after running on to the platform. They hurried to the dining car before all the seats were taken; once there, they gorged on eggs and bacon. In Soho the Minns were put up by a friend who valiantly vacated his bedroom and slept in a store cupboard for the night.

The Minns loved animals; they were often to be seen at the London zoo. They spent most of the time in the Small Mammal House, nudging their way through the other gapers and nibbling the nuts and fruit bought at the turnstile to feed the animals. They'd talk to the lemurs, genets and kinkajous in animal language, by imitating the noise each one made, oblivious of the crowd they attracted. Dorothy was in love with a small nocturnal creature usually curled asleep in its coop; it had a long ringed tail, a soft bushy pelt the colour of verdigris, button-black eyes, tiny round ears, and flexible snout like damp indiarubber. It answered to its name printed above the cage, and when called ran down from the coop and sat at the bars waiting to be scratched. Later, at home, Dorothy had to wash her hands free of the lingering foxy smell.

After eating a heavy dinner, Dorothy would often dream about the animal—she dreamed she was dressing it in swaddling clothes. The approach of their wedding anniversary, Minn asked his wife if there were anything special she craved—the answer he got was that animal in the zoo. The following week in London, Minn scoured the pet shops until he found one that offered to procure a similar creature from Mexico.

The day of the anniversary the animal had not arrived. The Minns spent the evening bickering. Minn went to bed at nine, Dorothy remained downstairs drinking and dancing a solo to Frank Sinatra on the phonograph.

Next morning Minn entered the kitchen in his red leather slippers.

'Wearing your skates,' said Dorothy, as he was always slithering about in them.

'That was such a good soup you made yesterday. And the roast was the best in a long while. Are there any left-overs?'

'You've just had breakfast, guzzleguts.'

'You're not such a bad feeder yourself, you know,' Minn defended himself. He was feeling shaky after a sleepless night. He had had one of his recurrent nightmares of his wife, dressed in bright tartan trousers, chasing him up the steps of his stuffy London club. The club was a great haven. Minn liked to spend the afternoon reading the newspapers in a deep armchair close to the coal fire, and have a footman bring him china tea and anchovy paste sandwiches. The instant Dorothy burst into the club and bawled him out in front of the other members, Minn awoke from the dream was a shout.

Later that day Minn came upon his wife in the process of packing a suitcase in the bedroom. She announced she was going to spend a few days with her mother.

Minn was alone when a letter arrived from the petshop. Gleefully he sprinted off to London. He had a fine time on his own. After an anchovy tea at the club he bought a green tweed suit at Fortnum and Mason. At the petshop he gave a cheque for thirty pounds and was handed a wicker basket with a black snout protruding through the wire in the front. The animal's diet was to consist of raw egg and banana; the shop gave him one of each for good measure.

Back in his friend's flat in Soho, Minn released the animal in the bathroom, then he took his friend to dine at the Savoy grill. They ate a grouse apiece, and ordered a vintage claret. In the taxi going back they smoked cigars. They got into the flat and found the bathroom in a state of pandemonium. The soap was indented with claw marks, the paper was ripped off its reel, a bottle of French bath essence was in fragments on the tiles, and it was clear the animal had not acquired any training. They had a job catching it; every time Minn approached to grab its tail the tiny creature squealed in terror and ran behind the lavatory base. As a final expedient Minn flung a towel over its head and they gathered it up that way. Next day the friend was not sorry to see Minn depart for the station. In the train the frenzied squeals coming from the wicker basket roused the interest of the other passengers. 'What dear little cat is that?' inquired an old lady, putting a finger through the wire and receiving a vindictive nip. Apologies followed. Someone complained of the smell and Minn moved to another compartment. He was very relieved to reach the outskirts of the town and the tunnel that preceded his station.

Minn had a great affinity with animals. Back in the country he carefully closed the kitchen door, took off his shoes and jacket, and put a banana and bowl of water on the linoleum. Minn was determined to have a rapprochement. He tenderly unlatched the clip of the basket and let the animal out again. It made a dash for the dresser, vanished underneath and remained there. She was so small and scrawny that Minn judged her to be about three months, and the raw place with the dabs of dried blood on the tail to have been caused by a trapper hitching her to a peg. Minn felt sorry for the poor little creature, but the more he coaxed the more reticent she became. So he gave up, quietly shut the door and went upstairs to work. All he managed to get done the next few days was the priming of one canvas. The animal stayed under the dresser and steadily lost weight. The banana on the linoleum went black. The butcher delivered a message to say Bessie was ill and could not quit her caravan. Exasperated, Minn called his wife. 'That boring old basket . . .,' her mother was saying as the telephone pealed.

'You'd better come back and cope. This place is an absolute shambles,' Minn said. It was pouring with rain as Dorothy walked into the house with a bag of sawdust under her arm.

'How many times did your mother call me a boring old basket?'

'No so many,' said Dorothy, and they laughed. Relations were resumed with a great resurgence of affection. Dorothy cleaned up the mess, she was in her element. Later they moved the furniture out of the dining room, hauled up the matting and stacked it in the garage. In the garden they found a dead tree stump, dragged it into the bare room and placed a coop on the top. Dorothy sprinkled the floor with sawdust. Then in thick oven gloves she fished under the dresser and brought out her squealing pet by the tail. It was dropped into its new home. 'Minny, Minny, Minny,' Dorothy called. Minny ran into her coop and remained there.

The following week Minny began to fill out while Dorothy haunted the dining room in thick oven gloves; every time she made a grab at Minny to pet her, there were piercing squeals of terror, with Minny crouched in a corner, her paws raised to protect her button-black eyes.

'Stop working off your aggression on that animal,' Minn shouted down from the studio.

'I'm training it,' Dorothy shouted back.

The Minns, like gloating parents, doted over Minny with increasing avidity. In the village they bought her delicacies like hothouse grapes, Basses-Alpes honey and peaches. They would stand beside the tree stump and study Minny squatted on her haunches with her tiny black paws like witch's stumps gripping the fruit as she munched. She had a way of tilting her head at an angle as if on the alert for the sound of approaching danger, and she moved about in a funny kind of humped trot. Also, she had a way of squatting and rubbing her muzzle with her paws and blinking in a short-sighted fashion. In the evenings when the light changed Minny chased the shadows, and sometimes she seemed to go berserk.

It was a month before Minny could be picked up without any piercing squeals, and one evening to Dorothy's delight of her own accord Minny came and nestled on Dorothy's lap.

April, on the first day of spring, Minny was about a year old. She had filled out considerably and developed quite a rump. It was a ravishing hot day. 'The best England can do,' said Bessie in between cleaning, as she glared across the meadows. There was not a breath of wind. Now that Minny was tame she used people's legs as tree stumps. They could pick her up ad infinitum and there were no more squeals of terror. 'Minny, Minny, Minny,' Dorothy called, leading the way into the garden. After being cooped up all winter Minny was delighted with her freedom and scampered out after her. The grass was moist and green, and the crocuses were up. Minny had no inclination to stray, it seemed. She liked company, and preferred to prowl close to the house as she snuffled about the grass with her flexible snout nuzzling for bugs and worms, or she'd climb the arbutus and swing from branch to branch like an acrobat.

Minn came into the garden wearing his pumps. 'It's no day for work,' he said, tilting his head at an angle as if on the alert. Whistling, Minn walked across the lawn to inspect the shrubs he had planted in the autumn. Minny vacated the tree and gave a flying leap to the grass, she ran up Minn's trousers and squatted on his shoulder, keeping herself balanced by clutching his soft wispy hair with her black witch's stumps. Minny loved flowers, at the sight of each bud she let out bird-like chirrups of pleasure and excitedly nipped Minn's neck just behind the ear.

Dorothy went back to the house and attacked the carpet, picking off the fluff that the sweeper had overlooked. Then she stood at the kitchen window and waited for Bessie to leave so that she could redo the housework.

'Don't forget to bring some more farm butter tomorrow,' Dorothy said, as glaring Bessie passed her and went out of the back door to straddle a bicycle with her gnarled black-stockinged legs. In the distance Minn was seen pottering about the daffodils in the shrubbery followed by two white geese and nine guineafowl.

'Hey! Watch out for the bulbs,' Dorothy shouted.

'Stop nagging, and what's for brunch?'

'It's ready when you are.' Dorothy laid a pillow and a blanket on the grass; she spread a cloth over the garden table and on it placed a dish of raw tomatoes stuffed with mayonnaise and shrimps, a roast chicken, a green salad, plates, glasses and home-made bread and butter. Minn sauntered back to the house with the geese and guineafowl in his wake.

'You know I can't stand those birds with their filthy droppings hanging about the back door for food.'

'I'm going to give them some bread, you've been starving them of late.' Minn disappeared into the house with Minny humped on his shoulder.

'Hey! Take off your pumps. The kitchen floor's just been twice scrubbed.' Demented, Dorothy grabbed a broom and ran out into the garden to lunge at the guineafowl. In the cellar Minn picked out a bottle of Chablis as he whistled happily, 'Oh! To be a million miles away. A million miles from here.' Minny ran down his leg and snapped up the spiders lurking in the cobwebby dark crannies. They returned to the garden and saw Dorothy, a bleached Valkyrie in shorts and suntop, flinging a broom after the receding birds. The ensemble vanished into the vegetable patch. Minn uncorked the wine and filled two glasses.

'You know Dorothy, you could be quite a nice person if you got yourself analysed. You could do it on the National Health scheme.' Minn was seated on the grass with a plate on his knee as he scrabbled at the chicken the way Minny beside him was dislodging date stones with her claws.

'I think you could do with a little analysis yourself, Minn.' Dorothy laughed, still a bit out of breath, her head tilted at an angle the way Minny held hers, and she picked some fluff off Minn's check rancher's shirt. 'You know, that privy would make a perfect summer residence for baby.'

A small window led from the privy to the top of a coal shed and Minny would be able to jump in and out and lie in the sun as much as she pleased, in the summer it would be less claustrophobic than the dining room.

'It looks the ideal prison, if that's what you mean.' Minn had finished eating, he walked humped fashion to the garage and brought out a length of wire, some nails and a hammer, and climbed to the top of the shed to get to work making a cage to coop Minny in, should they go out for the day. Dorothy walked humped fashion to the kitchen and cleared the debris.

'You're getting more like Minny every day,' Minn shouted down.

'Speak for yourself,' Dorothy called, 'I'm going to give baby a bath.' She grabbed Minny from the grass and hoisted her off to the bathroom. The tub was filled with water with a rubber duck and some sponges. Minny was lowered into the luke-warm water and smothered in egg nogg shampoo. She clung to Dorothy's hair and emitted a high-pitched squeal.

'Working off some more aggression,' said Minn, going sulkily up to his studio. He lay on the divan and faced the skylight, brooding. He felt in a gloom and mused on his childhood, his nanny and his carefree prep school days, until the sound of a lawnmower lulled him into a doze.

Minny was thoroughly rubbed and put in the sun to dry. At dusk Dorothy put the gardening tools away and went in search of Minny who was nowhere to be seen. 'Minny, Minny, Minny,' she called. There was no answering squeal. Dorothy walked round the garden and went on calling Minny. Suddenly, from across the fields a tiny dot appeared on the horizon, nearer and nearer it approached, and Minny her long bushy tail erect came bounding over the grass. 'Wicked baby,' Dorothy scolded, 'scaring me like that.'

That night Minny was allowed upstairs. She jumped on the bed and burrowed under the blanket. Dorothy was teasing her and rolling her over when Minn said,

'You're completely obsessed with that animal. All your mothering instincts go on it now instead of me.'

'Are you going to sleep in that dirty old rancher's shirt?'

'I don't want to get scratched.'

'You weren't thinking of that in the garden today.'

'Bed's different.' Minn turned his back and felt a nip through the sheet. Seizing his pillow he leaped out of bed, saying, 'It's that animal or me,' and went into his studio. From then Minn remained there, sleeping on the divan, while clean and silky Minny took over his half of the bed, and lay stretched out all night with her paws round Dorothy's throat.

Minny had a desperate need of affection, she never liked being left alone, as soon as she got in the house she'd dash full of purpose up the stairs to the bed where she knew Dorothy was bound to appear some time. If Minny got shut out in the garden, she'd clamber over the roof and ease a window open with her snout, determined to get in some way.

Minn emerged from the studio less and less. He was trying to sketch Minny, but was hampered by his wife's intrusions. It was always 'time for baby's bath', or 'Bessie won't do your room if baby's loose in the house.' Minny would be snatched up and dumped in her cage. One day Minn lost his temper and called his wife 'ajealousbitchgetout'. Bessie glared more than ever at having an extra bed to make. 'Is that lazy bugger up yet?' was her morning greeting, since the master's hibernation. Minn could hear her voice crackling up through the gaps in the rotting oak beams.

'What was it Bess called me?'

'A lazy bugger,' Dorothy repeated with relish.

'All we need is your mother here to call be a boring basket.' This time nobody laughed. Minn began to take solitary drives, it assuaged a spirit of rebellion and was a means of avenging himself on the shrews he felt were hemming him in. He would stride defiantly into the garage, rev up the open tourer and drive maniacally round the countryside. One autumn day he put Minny on the seat beside him and they tooled off together. They returned at dusk to find Dorothy having hysterics. She had telephoned the police and reported the car as stolen. Beating the top of her head, Dorothy boasted,

'The entire police force are out scouring the county for you.'

'Don't you have any heart?'

'I'm sorry I'm so vindictive.' Dorothy kissed him and they had a reunion over a bottle of rum in the crimson sitting-room. 'I'm so worried about baby,' Dorothy confessed.

'She gets cooped up enough.'

It's not that. But all this week she's been frenziedly leaping the branches and breaking off twigs to make nests in the trees. And yesterday she bit into a pillow and ran in and out of the house with swansdown between her teeth. Then she chased the geese into the next field and bit one in the wing. Clearly, she's in a terrible state of frustration. Poor baby's at an age to be mated.' Dorothy gave Minn a cold appraising stare.

'Good heavens! You don't expect me to do something about it, I hope,' he said nervously, and his laugh sounded more like a croak. But they went to bed like a normal couple for a change. Minny was there ahead of them, looking very angelic and silky.

'Do we have to have her in the bed? said Minn, getting into his best tangerine silk pyjamas. Minny was shoved to the bottom, causing her to wake with a start, as if from a bad dream. She sank her teeth into Minn's foot piercing the flesh to the bone. The sheet was soaked with blood and there was a prolonged wail of pain. Dorothy swathed his foot in a towel to arrest the flow, then they drove at a great speed across country to the nearest hospital to have the wound attended to.

They were sitting in the outpatients' ward when Minn said, 'Minny's got to go, you know. It's one shrew too many.'

Two weeks passed and the wound had not healed. Minn limped round the house on crutches, his whole leg inflamed. He was on his way to the hospital where he went twice a week for treatment. On the stairs he passed two women standing like sentinels, one hoisting a broom and the other with a dustpan. The women stood at the window to watch the master hobble across the lawn. He revved up the car and disappeared round the bend in the lane. One woman crouched down to the floor and picked some fluff off the carpet, the other went out of the house to straddle a bicycle.

Since the accident Minny had not been allowed out of her cage. Dorothy went into the garden and unlatched the privy, it was black and filthy inside, and for a moment it was impossible to detect poor baby asleep on a ledge in a corner. Dorothy dragged a hose from the garage and attached the nozzle to a tap. Minny was so delighted to see Dorothy she gave a flying leap, landed on Dorothy's shoulder and affectionately nipped her neck.

It was a sunny day with a very strong wind, the branches of the arbutus creaked and swayed in the breeze. Minny ran up the tree and swung from the branches until she spotted the approach of the geese. With a leap she hit the grass and gave chase, the geese turned about and squawking waddled away; the troupe vanished into the bushes. Hearing the noise Dorothy glanced out of the privy where she was busily hosing, a violent gust of wind blew the door to, the hose jerked out of her hand and the privy door slammed. There was no inside latch so Dorothy was trapped. A slit a foot across let in a faint ray of light. Now for a change Dorothy had a view of the kitchen window with smoke pouring out from the stew left on the stove. Now that their rôles were reversed, in between raids on the birds Minny kept coming back to see how Dorothy fared wedged in the tiny aperture shouting for help with the wind carrying her plea across the meadow. From the top of the shed Minny could reach down a paw and touch the windswept head. 'Help, Help, Help,' Dorothy called, and listened for the echo. Once a van hooted as it turned the bend in the lane. The telephone peeled several times. The stew boiled away and there was a smell of burning bones. Dorothy tried to break down the door, for hours she clawed at the tiny sill, her panic increasing at each unsuccessful attempt. It was raining before her spirit was broken, and everything had turned black so that she passed out altogether.

Overhead the guineafowl had gone to roost, and both the geese were dead, with Minny sated and comfortably asleep upstairs in bed before the master returned. Dorothy failed to recognize him. She was brought out clutching her head. She made no sense, but kept repeating, 'Has baby forgiven me?' Finally, a doctor came and took Dorothy away.

Early the following morning, still in his dressing gown, Minn hobbled down to the garage and brought out the wicker basket. Trusting little Minny was lowered into the basket with a banana and some grapes in case she were thirsty on the journey she was about to take. She clung to him desperately as if she already sensed her fate, and he had difficulty in disentangling her paws from his neck, before the clip of the basket was finally put in place.

Minn quickly dressed. Leaden with guilt he drove Minny to the station. Minn put the basket in the guard's van of the next train in, then he turned miserably away and limped out of the station.

Gloomsville

Friday Night man took the old lady's tit out of his mouth and stubbed it out in an ashtray.

'Can I come round for another hostility fix?' he said to Brune on the telephone at dawn on Saturday.

'What's up? Friday night's passed, you know.'

'The old lady's giving me luncheon. I thought I'd drop by later, though. If you're doing nothing, that is.'

Friday man donned a Chipp custom-made suit, decently well worn with stitched on leather elbow pads, the insignia of a Bostonian gentleman, set his khaki nutmeg hat size seven at a decent angle, and marched from the old lady's penthouse to the Racket Club on Park Avenue. Friday knew he dressed with scrupulous care to impress the old lady, and he tried to play it.

He was going to work off his aggression in the gym of the Racket Club, swiping the punch ball imagining it to be Brune. He had not behaved too well marching out on her in the Colony the previous evening. The old man wouldn't have approved. After all, he'd merely expressed an opinion that all women were whores; the English bloody; the French utterly decadent; and that all niggers started at Calais. Brune had snarled, 'I suppose it's just you and Mummy way out on a limb.' There was no need to get personal just because she disagreed. Friday had begun to feel lonesome. It was all very well living with the old lady, but at eighty-seven could she be considered the ideal companion for a man in his prime. Friday marched into a florist, wrote Mea Culpa on a card, and ordered some flowers. He marched back to the Racket and put his face under a sun lamp, three minutes either side. Later, he won a hundred dollars playing backgammon, his usual form on Saturdays.

The sky was blue. Sun glowed on the white walls, and glistened the china on the dresser as Friday entered Brune's apartment. Once a week steadily for a year he had been going there carrying a paper bag containing four beer cans. Friday placed three cans in the icebox. The fourth can he opened. He tipped in the beer so that no froth formed.

No matter the season Brune always greeted him in a leopard bikini. Orange hair fell to her bare shoulders and a clutter of anklets jangled as she stalked the apartment on pretty bare feet. Friday knew you could appease women with flattery, and said,

'You're looking very glamorous. Just like a goshawk.' An acquaintance at the Racket had initiated the meeting with Brune. It had been a way out party for Friday. He despised Manhattans. Loftily surveying the company he had opened the conversation. 'Quite an intelligent group here.' The most statuesque girl in the room Brune had pretty teeth and a sportive appearance he approved. Seated very close on a sofa, savouring the warmth of her body next to his, Friday only quit her side to replenish the drinks.

When not making explorations into the Venezualan jungle, the last ten years Brune had been writing a book on South American Indians. Her emotional life revolved round a succession of skunks and monkeys. The last had died of starvation. The present one, a woolly, although her growth was stunted, had survived six months.

Friday carried his glass across and squatted on the carpet. Ugly little beast! He scrutinized woolly's ribs as she jigged up and down whimpering pitifully, her scrawny arms dangling from the top of the excremented cage. 'Not dead yet?' Friday laughed. Brune was a challenge. He felt balanced on a precipice of rejection. It was a fresh experience. Women worshipped the ground he trod, though Friday suspected it was the family fortune they were after. He loved it here. It was a strange world in contrast to Gloomsville on Park Avenue. He felt relaxed surrounded by the harpoons, the medical supplies, the camera equipment, and the Indian spears. On the walls were sombre daubs of naked Indians and a portrait Brune had painted of herself as a white goddess with gypsy ear-rings. Scattered about the room were ball points and Alma Mater note books in which Brune was jotting her memoirs. A plucky woman, even he sensed that. She was organizing her third expedition into the jungle in search of diamonds. She had returned prematurely from the previous ones with minor minerals only. Supplies had run out, and some indispensable member of the team had quit, the engineer or the photographer, whomever Brune had chosen as her lover for that trip. Back in New York she related her experiences on a television programme called Girl Talk.

Friday marched on to a creepered terrace engulfed in late afternoon sunshine. There was the old skunk box still harbouring a rotted carcass.

'Mind your feet,' said Brune, as he entered the French window.

'Will do.' He marched back on to the terrace and scraped his shoes on a mat.

Friday had a particular fondness for the padded alcove where the bed stood. The old fashioned black teevee at it's base was reassuringly redolent of the nursery. He used to like to switch on and view some sporting event while making love. Otherwise he never got carried away, especially with Woolly perched above them on the bed rest.

'Where are the flowers I sent?'

'Yellow dahlias.' Brune's least favourite flora. She had stuffed the long spiky tentacles behind a curtain.

'They look like you. Spiders.' Friday looked pleased with himself. Swinging his arms he tiptoed to the icebox and extracted a fresh beer can.

'Don't sprinkle ash on the butter. And mind how you close it.' Brune followed. 'No, not like that.' Wasn't he hopeless. Too emasculated to give the icebox a firm slam. She thought of him as a child or an animal. He had a way of walking with short smart steps and swinging his arms military fashion with clenched fists and each thumb out like a flipper.

Brune never failed to be amazed how good Friday man looked, apart from the neanderthal hair cut like a clipped hedgehog to the touch. A pretty de-frocked priest with an all year round tan. She refrained from asking if he used a sun lamp. He would say it was beneficial to his health. 'I don't think I ought tonight with this virus, do you?' had been his farewell at the downstair door the last weeks.

Friday settled down piling the bright cushions into his back. He raised his socked feet on to the sofa. He would cop it if he put his shoes on the white cover. Friday thought of himself as a spoilt brat. He generated a self-deprecating assurance that tallied with this attitude. The more punishment he received the more flowers he sent. Plants as well. They poured in. Brune had made quite a friend of the florist who clambered up the stairs with them.

Friday had a way of rolling back his eyes until they vanished. When they returned from orbit he'd swing round to face Brune. She used to respond with, 'What beautiful green eyes you have.' The reaction was immediate. In five minutes they were bedded. Now as he did it she merely remarked,

'Given up smoking, I see.'

He was handling a pack of cigarillos. Changing his mind Friday defiantly put a filter tip in his mouth. 'Well, you force me to smoke these. You say you hate cigar fumes.'

'Still under the illusion you've given up smoking!'

'I'm too well adjusted to be effected by jibes of that kind.'

'Is that why you keep a black tit in your mouth?'

'Well, I did have a black Mammy as a kid. Perhaps that accounts for my taste in cigarillos.' He laughed.

'Was Mummy waiting up again last night?'

'Waiting for me to screw her,' Friday laughed. 'I'm only there for convenience, you know. To economize. You wouldn't talk the way you do if you realized what I'd been through . . . with my brother a fairy . . . and the other one married to a hooker . . . losing all my friends in the war . . . and being hospitalized after that. I wouldn't want Charlie Knickerbocker to hear. I don't know why I'm telling you all this suddenly. I must be in the bag. How about a little dividend on that?' He

pointed to her empty glass.
'Mind how you close the icebox.'
'Why don't you get it fixed? Is the toilet still not flushing?'
Brune had her goshawk look Was he going too far? Tomorrow he would send her some more spiders.
'I nearly bought you a coat this afternoon. Two hundred dollars. I knew I was in for another of manic bouts and got out of the store real quick. Not before I'd bought myself a watch, though. Like it? Only five hundred.'
'The trouble with you is you can't feel. Except for yourself.'
'Feel?'
'Exactly, don't know the meaning. Ever been in love?'
'I was so much in love with a girl once I saw her regularly once a week for three years. I was so much in love I was impotent. She worshipped the ground I walked on.'
'Why didn't you marry her?'
'The old lady wouldn't have approved.'
'How is the old lady?'
'I'm very worried about her. She' biting into capital. Quite soon there'll be nothing left. Of course, she should go on living in the manner to which she's acustomed. It's a bit tough, though, since the old man died. I'm having to look for a job. The old lady refuses to move into anything smaller. I found a gorgeous apartment half the price. But the doorman didn't wear white gloves, and the elevator wasn't perfumed. Nothing but an H-bomb will get her out of that penthouse . . . just as the old man said . . . she's nothing but a spoilt brat. I try to think what he'd do in my place . . . he was a real aristocrat . . . always had to have the best. He refused to go home unless driven by his own chauffeur. Know the derivation of posh?'
'No, and I don't want to.'
'I bet you don't know the two most important words in the English language? CHARGE IT. I'm dilettanti . . . only superficial

knowledge.'

'Mind where you put the beer.'

'As a kid all I wanted was to win the old man's respect. I was the crack yachtsman of my generation. He never gave me credit for it. I often used to wonder if I was his son . . . with the old lady roaming the corridors at night singing cockadoodle do . . . any cock will do. The beer's finished. I'll take you out for a snort if you like.'

'What about going to see *Long Day's Journey into Night?*'

'Too morbid.' Woolly was becoming increasingly plaintive. 'Why don't you give it some food?'

Brune unlatched the cage. 'My mother's instinct tells me it's had enough.' Woolly leapt out, straddled a spear and sidled to the ground. With distended arms lying on the floor on her back Woolly emitted a heart-rending wail just in front of the icebox. She was grabbed and buttoned into a red knitted jacket and tucked into Brune's waterproof.

'Care for a wing?' Friday's arm cricked ready to support her to the nearest bar. The bar was full. Friday ordered a Miller's High Life and a daquiri.

On the bar stool, propped against a vase of pussywillows in the corner, Brune debated whether this was the moment to once more suggest he invest in her forthcoming expedition.

'Is that a Chipp tie? It's pretty.'

'No, but thank you.' Friday beamed. Praise was scant from Brune. 'I often wonder why you see me. I'm not very nice to you.'

'Not nice to me! I'm lonesome. I'm completely at ease with you. I can say anything that comes into my head. You're my glamorous goshawk. I'm as much in love with you as I'm capable of being.' It gave him pleasure to say it. 'When the old lady's found me a position on Wall Street I'll be able to look after you, and help you with your expedition. You need someone like me to look after you. Now that the old man's dead I've got to marry in order to carry on the line.'

'Four people have already put up 10,000. I only need another ten,' said Brune, moved by his ingenuousness. The first month with Friday she thought she had met Tarzan. Brune was gazing into his green eyes when the bar lights dimmed. It was the hour the professionals filed in. Six of them. Tall blondes with flowing bleached hair, and a dumpy one with a Beatle wig.

'How do you like those apples!' Friday was excited. 'Is that a wig she's wearing? Those hookers get what they can out of you. But everyone needs all the money they can get. I'm rather indiscriminate. So long as I get satisfaction. Excuse me,' he slipped from the stool. 'Know the derivation of TIP. To Insure Promptitude.' He smiled like a clever little boy. Friday marched to the jukebox and waited for Dumpy's breasts to charge into him. Aware of each other they pressed close to the machine, and without looking up or speaking rammed home the same Bossa Nova knob. Wrap round skirts excited Friday. He wanted Dumpy. She wouldn't cost more than ten dollars. Exultantly, he placed twenty dimes into the slot and turned for her to press into him. The bar was dark. He could have shoved his hand into her wrap around and no one would have been the wiser. Pleased with himself Friday marched back to his beer. Woolly was having a fine time dipping her claws into the glasses and extracting slithers of lemon peel. A crowd had gathered, Woolly was being encouraged to snap up a saucerful of peanuts. Brune was raging.

Friday said, 'Too many jews in here.'

At the downstair door, he said,

'Think about what I've said. Time you settled down.' He marched thumbs up to the corner and hailed a cab.

'Cock a doodle do . . .' A small white-haired old lady was stomping the passage on squat swansdowne trotters. She was clasping a hypodermic and a pink Easter bunny with a daisy in its mouth.

'How's Miss Belsen?' the old lady's orbs were flaming.

'Now then Mom. The old man wouldn't care to hear you talk that way.'

'You're on another of your benders ... about to do something foolish. Miss Belsen'll make a monkey out of you yet.'

'I'm old enough to look after myself I'm forty-four next month.'

'You're on another of your bouts. I''ve booked you with the doctor at nine. Go to bed.'

'Will do.' Friday went past the old lady, cocked his hat at a decently defiant angle and marched out. Back at the bar stool he ordered a Miller's High Life. He scanned the bar stools until his eye alighted on Dumpy's breasts. Two hours later he groggily replaced the key in the latch.

The old lady still haunted the sittingroom. Friday tiptoed to bed. In the morning he dressed with care and turned up punctually at the doctor's. His manic attacks led to bouts of unwarranted high spending. Again thorazine was prescribed. Reminded of the florist bill Friday considered he'd got off lightly.

At breakfast Friday popped a thorazine into his coffee; he took another between meals; in the evenings he put another in his beer. His mother disguised more tablets in the food. Friday remained doped on thorazine, sipping beer slumped in a wing armchair before the dogwood fire the rest of the winter. Infrequent flickers of sunlight penetrated the neo-gothic windows of the dark sittingroom filled with potted azaleas trumped in whit satin ribbons. Like an assiduous wife Friday marched round emptying ashtrays and reviving the dying embers. If he talked it was with great volubility. Often about Brune.

There she was in the jungle. A white goddess lording it over those South American head hunters. In her leopard bikini, her hair flowing over a stream as she shifted gravel hoping to come upon a diamond. Paddling a canoe with the chief tribesman nude but for an anklet and a spear. Friday knew Brune's abortive explorations were a vain attempt to gain esteem from her dead mother whom as a child she had adulated. He understood Brune. Once while the old lady was having one of her after-meal snoozes he dialled Brune's number. There was no reply.

The spring holiday his brother came home from a little known Upstate University. Friday sobered up. The manic bout subsided. His brother took over the wing chair by the fire, and every night pooped out on brandy. During the day Friday absconded the building.

Central Park was five minutes' walk from the penthouse. He'd sit on one of the granite boulders and watch the ugly people passing, or he'd daydream clutching an unread yachting journal. It was still nippy. No buds were out. Friday wore a Harvard muffler. He did not join the squealing mob at the sealion pool. He did not ride a pony cart. He did not buy a pirate flag, a balloon, frankforters, pinwheels or peanuts from the barrow outside the children's zoo. He did not bring bread to feed the pigeons and squirrels. Sometimes he paused at the elk cage, the elks had their heads tilted at a disdainful angle and reminded him of his glamorous goshawk. Mostly, he enjoyed sitting on a bench at the skating rink, facing a line of skyscrapers. It was peaceful protected by the truncheoned police patrolling the area, shaded by rocks and a clump of blooming forsythia. Music played. Sun glistened the brow of the negro instructor, and the bald heads of the white-booted skaters.

The first of April the skating season terminated. Friday shifted his beat to the terrace of the cafeteria. He drank beer mooning up at the red balloons caught in the branches of the plane trees. Now and then he marched to the Men's Comfort Station and took a leak.

One afternoon a voice said, 'What a ducky tan. Get it sitting here?' It was Dumpy.

The end of the week Friday fished out a wrap around he kept hidden in the rear of the closet. He marched to Dumpy's bar. His eyes sought Dumpy's breasts. An hour later he was feeling them. Dumpy lay on her back stripped but for her Beatle wig and wrap around. Friday man was ditto.

'Youm! Youm!' he said, kissing her, and smacked his lips. 'Do you like being hugged?' He drew Dumpy to his glabrous chest and squeezed. Her respiration blocked, she gasped,

'Very much. What colour are your eyes?'
'Green.'
'Beautiful green eyes.'
He gave Dumpy's nipple a vicious tweak. 'Like that?' he hissed. His other hand caressing his own nipple, Friday goaded, 'Give us some action.' He was so pleased with Dumpy's pumping he gave her an extra ten dollars.

'How about trying it in a nun's outfit? It suits me,' she said.

Friday was definitely interested, but commented, 'I'm too well adjusted for that. I'll drop by next week, though. Be sure you're dressed so. Or I may not get my rocks off.'

He felt groggy as he put the key in the door at three in the morning. 'Cock a doodle do . . .'

'Now then, Mom. Like some nut fudge out of the icebox.'

After the doctor at nine o'clock Friday went direct to confession.

Doped on thorazine Friday was seated on the terrace of the cafeteria next to two dark-goggled women, a thin one and a fat one with flowing orange hair. The fat one's arms bulged in curdled folds over the rim of a sleeveless dress. A very tiny monkey lay asleep on her lap. A ball point and an Alma Mater pad were on the table. The orange heads intermingled, engrossed in themselves, oblivious of the outside world. They talked of the books each had been engaged on for years; should they combine on a typist to write for them; how there wasn't a pecker in the city; what men there were weren't men but monkeys.

The fat one got up to fetch more hot whipped cream chocolate, Virginia ham with yams and mashed potato. Her friend said,

'Like some help with the starch?'

'My mother always said I was too skinny.'

'She should see you now.'

Every now and then their conversation was interrupted by a group of children with stacked plates held precariously over Friday's neck. Pressing into him they leaned across and cooed at the monkey as it reached up with plaintive outstretched arms. The fat girl lifter her Alma Mater pad. Rising, she said, angrily,

'That's how the last got poisoned.'

Friday rose simultaneously and marched back through the park behind them, thinking what scum came into the park these days, and how soon he would find a nice girl to marry and carry on the line.

What's New?

Young Weingorse gave the impression of being a busy man. He acted with gusto. Whether he was eating or scanning a newspaper he did it with a splurge. In a tight dark suit he'd leap the stairs three in a bound and burst into a room like a bull entering an arena only to stand as if dazed by the sun, confronting a barerra behind which a protagonist lurked. He now faced his wife who lay supine, spreadeagled on the bed, the manner in which he caught her on his return from the office every evening. She was becoming a pain in the arse.

'What's new today, Helene?' She did not reply. So he grilled, 'Come on, girl. Give us some news.' He knew only too well she had nothing to impart. It put him in a doldrum right away. Sweeping a broad white hand across his brow he smeared to and fro gathering up sweat particles into a black acid blob which he transferred to the other hand, and smoothed from one outstretched palm to the other as if testing a fresh kneading process. Meanwhile, he tried to think up a menial task that would get his wife out of the havoc-ridden bed and into the basement.

Panic-striken, Helene stared back and mused, 'Now whenever I look at that man all I can see is a very small brass door knob.'

She handed him his trilby. 'Put on your hat and let me have a look at you.'

Weingorse was back in the office, reminiscing, his lips silently framing the words 'roast duck' over and over.

'Do stop mumbling on about your raw stock.' The remark did not penetrate. Instead, he pursued,

'What are the plans for this evening? I hope you've asked an amusing crowd in.' Was he going to have to spend another evening alone with this woman! What had he landed himself with! Perhaps he might bait her out of bed with the offer of a cinema? 'Seen *Guys and Dolls*, sweet creature? It's being revived at the Classic.' He quirked down at his plump wide fingers drumming the brief case, his lips pursed until they disappeared so that he resembled a sad sullen bird whose nest had been fouled by a cuckoo.

Helene had given up asking friends to dinner. Afterwards her husband always remarked, 'What use were that group to my business!'

With an effort she pulled on her dressing gown and blue bunnyscuff slippers. Hugging the bannister she stepped down the five flights to the kitchen. At the bottom she called brightly,

'I saved a nice end of garlic sausage for you.'

Weingorse was already groping inside the frigidaire. 'What happened to the rollmop here yesterday?'

'That damned abortionist bag,' Helene hissed, tripping over the brief case that his rear hid from view. 'Do take care where you put it.'

'Who's been at my kosher margarine?'

'Your mother looked in again today, inspecting the bins to make sure nothing had got into them.'

He frowned. Helene had another disturbing vision of a tiny brass doorknob. 'Tra la la. Here we go,' she thought, stoking the spluttering black boiler.

'Isn't it time you found us a servant to clean the house properly?'

'Not on the money you provide, honey.' As she spoke the lights fused. What had he done to deserve this! With lopping arms swinging in unison he covered the stairs three in a bound until he reached the drawingroom. Weingorse burst in and grabbed the telephone. He dialled the numbers of Bobby, Dick and Boozy. 'What's new, old boy. Done anything gay lately?' To Sonia, Jennifer and Jane, he asked, 'What's new, old girl. Anything on for this evening? Come! Tell! Do! I can't wait.'

At the end of the day Weingorse retired with a croaking voice unable to phrase another sentence. 'Cleaned your feet?' said Helene, in a final attempt at conversation. The response was a limp flick of the wrist, as much as to say, 'Out of my sight, woman.'

Both arms circling the pillow, his lips parted to emit the persistent drone rising to a roar and terminating in a throttled hiccup that blew out the pelmets and left them quivering, Weingorse sank into blissful oblivion. Helene took a tuinol and stuffed her ears with pink wax orodents.

At the usual hour the following evening as she heard a vehicle brake to the kerb Helene swung her legs out of bed and stood at the window to glimpse the familiar fat hand gripping the taxi rail.

Downstairs, she exclaimed, 'I've built a fire in the drawingroom. It's cheered up the place no end.'

Was she becoming extravagant? 'Hallo,' he said, flatly, 'What's cooking?'

'Nothing special.'

'Anyone telephoned?'

'I've been out most of the day.'

'My mother tells me you took a taxi back with the shopping.'

After dinner Weingorse rapped his knuckle on the newly marbled mantleshelf, his face posed into a smile while his lozenge eyes remained dead pan. Each time the telephone rang his expression unfroze. 'No! You don't say! Fascinating! Tell more! Do. Is it true they were having an affair in 53 or 2. Come! Tell! I can't wait.'

Weingorse dined less and less at home. His wife's allowance cut down, the little housekeeping that had to be done he entrusted to his mother. In an effort to economise on restaurants he sometimes brought home a business colleague. His mother set the reproduction Hepplewhite dining table with empty sauce boats and silver plated candelabra. She served his favourite sausage, meatballs, carraway bread and cheesecake. Helene was asked to leave the drawingroom free on those evenings. The morning after as soon as her husband's taxi had turned the bend Helene stole into the kitchen to pick at the remains, her mother-in-law appeared in the cellar to retrieve the kosher fats Helene had chucked in the dust bin.

Some evenings Weingorse brought back his father, and the two men played piquet. His mother cooked them Weiner Schnitzel.

'There's no one can cook for like you, Mamma.'

'How's your wife's cooking?'

'That thorn in my flesh.'

'Why did you marry the girl in the first place?'

'Why?' Weingorse clutched his head, 'If she'd asked me to kill Pappa I'd have done it. I was out of my mind.'

'Poor boy! Now we must make the best of it.'

Helene fell into the habit of going into the Mews to the Queens Head. A friendly publican called, Jo, greeted her. 'Hallo there, stranger,' he'd say, as if he missed her on the days she hadn't come in.

Jo would get one of his regulars to offer Helene a drink. The saloon door was always left open. From the street Jo's corpulent frame could be seen sprawled across the bar, his elbows propped against the beer pumps, and his head slumped forward like an enormous beached fish.

Jo had a friend, William, who came into the pub every evening. William confessed to Helene that ever since his wife's demise he'd had a run of shocking bad luck. Due to eye trouble he'd lost his job as a chauffeur with the Daimler Hire Company. Referring to each one by a christian name he said he missed driving the movie stars to Brighton for weekends, they gave such smashing tips. Since then he'd lost one job after another. Here he was on the loose again. William showed her photographs of his late wife in a kimono serving tea, and of himself in white tie and tails being presented with the first prize for a ballroom competition. Helen asked, Can you cook? Shovel klinker? Wait at table? Mix drinks? Mend? Press? and shop? Was she thinking of a full time position, living in. If so he'd start right away, providing he was given three months' wages in advance to pay for his wife's tombstone.

Young Weingorse reckoned what he'd spent on restaurants the past months and agreed to employ William.

William moved in. One day William said, 'What about Dolly?' He felt lonely not having the bitch with him. Helene converted a basement cupboard into a kennel, and forbade the mongrel access to the upstair rooms.

Now whenever Helene went into the kitchen it was filled with loafing tradesmen drinking tea and chatting in rhyming slang. The upstair part of the house seemed bleak in comparison, and she'd sit with them.

Their first dinner party Helene helped William who had grown a black moustache and side burns, and looked very Balkan in a striped apron and chef's cap. Each time the door bell rang to announce the arrival of a guest a muffled bark rose from the cellar.

Helene stood in her Bunnyscuffs in the store pantry and pushed the dishes through the hatch. The floor above William hauled up the trolly. 'Coming up.' Helene called through the trap.

'O.K. mate. Let her go.' William shouted down.

Their guests seated at the dinner table William poked his head into the aperture and observed, 'A couple of ginger beers up here, mate.'

The first course was soup. William had difficulty in keeping the plates steady.

'I hope after this we're not going to have a wine sauce with the fish, at any rate,' the host complained.

Between courses William shouted, 'The Governor's finished. Next one up, mate.'

The main course was stuffed cold veal in brown batter with rounds of goose eggs. Her husband's favourite. With it Helene took her place at the table. At each chill mouthful her anxiety increased. If a guest addressed her she gazed blankly at the rotating mouth of the speaker, unable to take in what was said. The mozzarella in front of him Weingorse beamed, 'Very tasty,' and went on dynamically dominating the conversation.

What's New?

By the time William had cleared the silver plate and flicked the crumbs off the table the host was in a dreamy sullen mood. Rapping his knuckles on the shiny mahogany he reflectively focused on the mannerist painting above his head. Before leading the guests upstairs he went over and tenderly straightened it.

Attracted by the voices Dolly broke loose. She romped up to and gained attention by rolling about the Aubusson with her paws in the air. The women roped in pearls and black crêpe seated on the mud brown satin settee took turns bending over Dolly and tickling her tits. Suddenly, with a vicious growl Dolly dashed to the velvet curtain and ripped off two dangling white bobbles.

Each time Weingorse rushed at her shouting, 'Get out of here, will you?' Dolly found an occasion to slip in again. Conversation was impossible.

Helene handed round the coffee. As she passed Weingorse hissed, 'Gush! Gush more! Can't you?' or 'Your hair's in a fearful mess.' 'Couldn't you have put on something more decollete.' or 'Must you wear brown shoes with a black dress!'

The after dinner guests began to arrive in droves out of taxis. The telephone peeled incessantly. Thirsty spongers had got wind of a party and were ringing in the hope of a last minute invitation.

Helene slipped away to join William for a quickie in the Queens Head.

Weingorse had his lickerish eyes on the door when his wife came back. 'What's your game?' he blurted, 'Don't you know the cigarettes have run out?'

Helene gulped down more tranquillizers with her brandy, and joined the junior partner, a young ginger man with a stutter who had invested all his capital in Weingorse Cement Mixers. Helene became very animated. She ridiculed his voice, and he pretended to like it. They appeared to be enjoying themselves when Weingorse went over and violently elbowed his wife off the couch. In a far corner, he hissed,

'Come off it, will you! Talk to Crabclaw. We need him for business.'

The party over Helene said, 'Who was that pretty blonde you spent the whole evening with?'

'Thought you'd make a fool of me with the junior partner. Eh!'

'Afraid I'd spill the beans that our honeymoon came out of his capital?' They had a fisticuff fight standing over broken glasses, cigar stubs, drink dregs and empty whisky bottles. Weingorse went to bed and sobbed. 'What have I done to deserve this?'

In the morning released from the coal cellar Dolly ran round the house leaving a trail of ghostly paw marks. A cleaner had to be summoned to do a rush job on the brocade.

Helen began to feel persecuted. The telephone would peel, she'd lift the receiver only to hear heavy breathing and the line go dead. Outside parked against the kerb a man sat stubbornly at the wheel of an Austin Seven. Each time Helene left the house he revved and grated along in low gear a few paces behind her. She gave him the slip by turning abruptly and walking back. She'd listen to the screech of brakes and watch the car swerve round, then she'd dart down a side street.

After a week a new character appeared in front of the telephone booth. A small man stood all day gazing up at the bedroom window. Helene pointed him out to William. Once William waved, and the man winked back.

Helene's mother-in-law haunted the house more and more. One afternoon she burst into the bedroom while the two of them were spring cleaning.

'The junior partner asked after you today,' Weingorse said one evening, laying down his newspaper.

Helene glared. 'Why doesn't your mother just put a bed in the hall and sleep there.'

By ten o'clock the telephone had abated, but no dinner was served. Helen went down to the kitchen to investigate the smell wafting up the stairs. She found William asleep with his feet on the table, and whisky on his breath. The vegetables were stewed to charcoal pellets.

'Helene,' Weingorse stressed. 'This isn't fair. It's simply not fair.' She had to agree. 'What's more,' he sobbed, 'William's never been any good as a servant. It must be the first time he's tried a hand at it. Three days now and no clean shirt. Also, I don't care for the way he sneers over the breakfast tray. It's up to you to retrieve the advance wages.'

Later that night Weingorse was elbowing his secretary along the platform as they ran to catch the night train to Birmingham.

Helene returned from a visit to her mother bearing in mind three heartening remarks repeated endlessly throughout the weekend.

'Give it time.' 'It takes time to settle down to marriage.' 'Only time can tell.'

Helene was determined to carry out her good resolutions. Carrying a suitcase, a dozen eggs, an azalea and two jars of her mother's crabapple jelly loosely wrapped in a package, she took a bus from the station. She mounted the stairs with renewed buoyancy. On the third floor she picked up the telephone. The other end of the line Boozy's ripe voice said,

'What's new, old boy?'

On the floor above, talking into the extension, her husband exclaimed, 'New! I'll tell you what's new. I've had enough.'

'Of what? Old man.'

'I've been robbed. All the drawers are empty. Everything's topsy turvy. Never seen anything like it. All my new shirts missing. The old ones as well. All my suits, brand new pinstripes, and all the others too. Pyjamas, ties, socks, the lot. Nothing but shoes in the cupboard. What have I done to deserve this? On top of which nothing's insured. After all, it's not as though I were Charlie Crabclaw. Eh! Old boy.'

'Certainly not. It's Helene's fault. You should teach that girl a lesson. Has she put a bulb in the hall? I came a cropper on the mat the other night.'

Helene jabbed down the receiver and ran into the basement.

'What was that? Sorry, old man. Call you back.'

'My advice is. Call the police.'

'I shall certainly get on to my lawyer.'

William's dark boxey room was deserted. The curtain was still drawn. The cupboard open and bare. Hangers lay on the floor and beside the unmade bed amongst the stubs on the chair was an empty whisky bottle. Dog food had congealed on a plate in front of the gas fire. Propped against a squeezed out tube of toothpaste was a folded note on which was written, 'The Governor propositioned me. Tootleooh mate.'

Helene was sitting up at the bar of the Queens Head. She hadn't been back to the house. During the week she'd had one glimpse of her husband, the brief case under his armpit as he thumbed a taxi in Bond Street.

Helene lifted her glass of bitter lemon and gin and turning to Jo, smiling, she said, 'Down the hatch.' Jo raised his tankard. 'Here's mud in your eye.' Jo went on polishing the glasses, giving her furtive glances from between his small puffy lids. 'Your husband gave him fifty quid to compromise you. Wasn't going to get mixed in any monkey business, William said. Then went off to the dogs with the money, and blew it. Came here next day and left a dud cheque . . . known the man twenty years . . . a dud cheque after all that time. Course . . . we do get a lot of duds in this business. But, after all, Helene . . .' Jo went on polishing, looking up to see how she was taking it, wondering if he was being too familiar. 'You know, Helene, I must say I wouldn't have expected it of William.'

'Poor William. I suppose he'd had his bout of bad luck for too long.' Helene laughed in a mood of joyful good humour.

Jo came from behind the bar and helped her on with her overcoat. Winking, he did it up tightly to the neck as far as the buttons would go.

'I won't be able to get out of it now.' Helene shook with laughter. Still laughing she picked up her suitcase. 'See you,' she said, and passed through the bar into the Mews.

She crossed the street heading for the corner chemist who kept her stocked in blue bombs, Miltowns and Orodents. That done she walked back and fumbled for the key in her bag. With a thumping heart she unlocked the door and tiptoed in.

Her husband stood naked in the bedroom talking sotto voce into the telephone.

'I'll tell you what's new, old boy. My wife's back.' He took a step forward, his shoulders hunched, and his head sunk forward.

In a tone of forlorn surprise, he muttered, 'It's late, Helene. Where have you been?'

'Alright,' she said, as if to reassure him.

'I didn't sleep all night.'

'You didn't?'

His body sagged and went limp, the bellicose expression faded. He stood without moving, in a state of abject collapse, mute, transfixed, staring down, infantile, and he whimpered. The dynamo had run down. Helene was moved. He's utterly wretched, she thought, and watched him horrified. His life was ebbing away. His mouth opened several times like a dying bird's beak waiting for the succour it knows it will never receive. Then he collapsed on the carpet at her feet.

'It's all my fault,' she said, 'I must be a witch.' She crouched down and stroked his head. Did she love him, after all? A doctor, she asked.

'I was like this in the office today. Mamma. Pappa,' he whispered. Crawling crab-wise toward the dresser he reached into a drawer to extract a pyjama bottom but collapsed half way. Rigidly paralysed and groaning, globules of sweat had risen to the tips of the dark hair on his back like a covering of hoar frost.

Helene telephoned his parents. His mother answered.

'What is the matter?'

'He's groaning.'

'What happened?'

'He collapsed.'

'When was this?'

'When I came in.'
'When was that?'
'Just now.'
'But, it's late.'
A trap? A cruelty charge, perhaps?

Pappa was trembling as he mounted the stairs. 'What's the matter with my son?' 'What's he eaten?' said Mamma, 'How's his stomach?'

They were resigned. There was no reproach in their tone. The parents dragged him into bed and pulled his pyjamas on. His mother prepared a hot water bottle. They sat silently waiting for an hour or more.

Suddenly young Weingorse's beak opened, 'I'm finished,' he said. 'Destroyed. I've lost my self respect . . . I'm dropped by serious people . . . such great hopes . . . now I'm a laughing stock . . . I want to live . . . To be happy . . . no one has respect anymore. No one takes me seriously . . . The firms gone downhill. Crabclaw's backed out. I'm ruined . . . destroyed. Who's paying for my trip to the States?' He went on at great length.

'Poor boy! Think yourself lucky you've no babies.' Pappa smoothed his son's hand. The crisis was over. Helene had a vision of a very small brass doorknob.

Nobody noticed her slip away. She hadn't eaten for days. Down . . . down . . . down she went to the basement. She soft-boiled two eggs. Her feet on the kitchen table she ate the eggs with thin slices of brown bread and butter. Another try? Who knows? The eggs were good. She thought of nests and eggs. The spring. Helene rocked back and forth in the chair. Nests and eggs. Yes! One day she'd have something new for him! Just wait. He'd see. . . . Laughing, she rocked back and forth in the chair. She'd have news for him yet.

Nutty as a Fruit Cake

Benny St Clair's ground floor apartment on the West Side was the setting of a newspaper tycoon. Stacked against the slate grey walls were old copies of the *Herald Tribune*, *New York Times*, *World-Telegram*, *Journal America*, *Daily News*, *Mirror* and *Pictorial*. Corners were filled with carboard cartons containing *Time* and *Life* magazines, *Harper's*, *Atlantic* and the *New Yorker*, and every other periodical printed during the past fifteen years. It looked an editorial hoard of a lifetime.

Perched on the piles of printed matter were black-hooded strip lamps casting an eerie glare. The desk was carefully arranged with fresh-sharpened pencils, pens, inks, stamping gadgets, index cards, file boxes and staples, like any well-stocked stationers. Next to a tape recorder and a telephone was a typewriter, a thermo fax and deodorant machine, its fan ridding the room of bad odours; and above the desk, pulled down low, was a long strip of fluorescent lighting. Scattered about the room were open boxes of Kleenex and cigarette cartons. The shelves were filled with books on world affairs, encyclopedias and dictionaries. Little daylight ever entered the apartment, and a gigantic drainpipe loomed into view from the windows. It was as if one had entered a literate troglodyte's cavern.

Benny referred to himself as an Independent Research Company. A small, spry man, tough in appearance, with a college crew-cut and soft pulpy lips in the shape of cupid's bows, he moved with a jaunty swing.

Benny flourished a cigarette holder and a green plastic cup as he passed through the dim lit hall to the kitchen to tot up with more powdered coffee from the Choc Full o' Nuts jar. He must have drunk at least ten cups throughout the course of one evening.

Benny resumed his position on a swivel stool opposite his desk and pivoted round, his eye narrowly missing a TV antennae. I was sitting impeccably dressed in a green suede suit on a small low couch with its oxblood slip cover from Bloomingdale's, my pointed patent toes rested sedately on the little plastic mat that separated us. I had been concentrating on Benny's movements all evening, following the squelch of his slippers as he padded about the kitchen, and listening to the uninterrupted flow of water flushing the sink; I was too shy to question the reason.

Benny laid down another drink. I thanked him and flicked away the coaster adhering to the glass each time I raised it; I was not too shy to mention it was over-diluted. In a bound Benny had vacated the swivel stool and hurried to the kitchen to add another jigger of whisky.

'You're too nice,' I said. I laughed, adding, 'That's your trouble. Too nice.' The point being I was morbidly masochistic. His bright grey eyes glinted.

'Once in a while I like to please a broad. Don't think you're going to change me.' His reply instilled some doubt as to his niceness and exacerbated my interest. It was the third evening in succession that Benny had invited me to his apartment for a drink; each time he had telephoned round seven, and I had immediately accepted. Benny made a point of not drinking, not any more; coffee was his only stimulant, so he said; and every morning he swallowed a mood brightener called Niamid, that he recommended everyone should take.

Tense moments passed with the two of us sitting as though transfixed, occasionally reversing the rôles of a rabbit and a snake; Benny perched on the stool as he gulped coffee and inhaled one filter tip after another, until a sufficient number of stubs had accumulated to tilt into the waste bin, and I on the couch with a drink as I listened to some monologue. There was no subject on which Benny did not speak as an authority; facts poured out of him; I was impressed, but nothing he said interested me much. His mind was like a machine; he was very matter of fact; also, he had unflinching opinions, such as—all homosexuals were treacherous and could never be trusted, that Katherine Mansfield lacked a mind, and the best way to cook aubergine was with sugar.

He claimed to believe there was a logical solution to everything; once you had control of the emotions the course of your life would run on an even keel—it only required reason and discipline—or so he had been saying for three evenings. Once you knew th cause of an intense feeling, just apply reason and discipline—you need never suffer irritation or unhappiness. This was a rational unromantic speaking.

'Discipline,' Benny repeated, 'I've mastered it. Married six times. Six times,' he repeated, as if he could not quite give it credence. 'Who needs women! I need them like I need a hole in the head.' He chuckled. 'Don't think I'm not well out of it now, though. My! The third. That was a nut for you.'

I had heard about the first two the previous evening. So compulsively had Benny reminisced, it was early morning before, groggy with fatigue. I had been able to heave myself from the apartment into Eighth Avenue where the bums had just emerged from the subway and were adjusting their rags prior to raking through the garbage left on the kerb for the dawn trucks to empty.

Benny had not offered to see me home, he had hinted it would be imprudent for him to quit the apartment, an important call might come along, although his telephone had not sounded all the evening.

'What was the third wife like?' I was curious.

'Was she nutty? A big juicy blonde. It was during the war I married that broad. As soon as I went overseas she wrote saying she wanted a divorce. She seemed real scared of being alone or something, and moved to Florida with her mother. They had an interest in a chain of hotels there. Mad for jade, that one. Returning home on leave, I stopped off and bought her a bit. A ring. She never put that ring on her finger. Blew her top each time I mentioned jade.' Benny was thoughtful. 'It was after that leave the baby was born. When I got back to my ship, again she wrote saying she wanted a divorce. I got permission to return and see what was bugging her. By chance I stopped off at the jade joint. There was the ring that I'd bought, returned to the shop.' Benny was baffled.

'Why should she want to do that, do you think?'

'To get back the money, I'd have thought.'

'She had no need of money. Was her mother loaded! When I challenged the broad about it, she raised the ruddy rooftops. To appease her I fixed myself up with a base job in Boston, went up there and looked for a house for us. When I got back to Florida she had some screwball hanging about after her. I packed her and the baby on to the train for Boston. During the night the two of them vanished. The coach attendant searched everywhere. Where do you think we finally found the dame? In the men's room, drinking.' Benny laid down his holder, with apparent satisfaction he thumbed out the stub and tilted the litter into the waste bin; his manner suggested that in a similar fashion he had rid himself of that broad. Gleefully he chuckled,

'Never again. Not this one!' rose and swung into the kitchen, to return with his cup held at an angle of triumph.

'What happened to the fourth wife?'

'Was she nutty? I awoke one night to find her bending over me with a stiletto. She was a ballerina, that one. You couldn't get me to sleep with another woman for two years after that episode. I never wanted to marry any one of them. Badgers, the lot. I'm still friendly with the last, though. But spoilt. An actress. She was used to men drinking out of her slipper.' He jabbed at his chest with the holder. 'But not this one! She's just flipped to shack up with a Cuban. A waiter twenty years younger than herself. I tell you! Can anything be nuttier than that! No one could say that broad wasn't well lubricated. Now I stick to my literati lady friends. But who needs women!' Again it was three in the morning. Was he never going to come to the point? Unable to be receptive to another word, I stuck out my neck and said,

'I'm tired. Do you think I might stay here tonight?' I was desperate, and the whisky helped. Benny did not betray surprise, but he did stop talking and leap from the swivel chair, saying, 'Here we go!' In a matter of fact manner he pulled out the couch to convert to a bed.

Benny brought fresh sheets, with a clean pair of pyjamas for himself and a clean pair for me. An interminable time seemed to pass, while the sound of swilled water penetrated the silence of the dim-lit hall. Would it never stop? Benny reappeared radiating hygiene, and chewing a strand of dental floss. We settled in back to back. I awaited some gesture of desire or affection—anything—but it never came. I lay hardly daring to breathe, I was so afraid of disturbing him, and had difficulty getting to sleep. During the night, by accident our bodies touched; I reached out a hand, and Benny grabbed me. Afterwards, he said,

'I've been awaiting you all night like a predatory animal.' I combed my hair. Benny disappeared to the bathroom. The performance was not repeated. In the morning, as soon as he opened his eyes, Benny lit a cigarette and went about his business at a brisk pace. On went the water for the coffee and the flow in the kitchen resumed. The newspapers were collected from the mat. Benny dressed and settled to work on the swivel stool in the glare of the fluorescent light; there he operated all day, sometimes without a break, so engrossed did he become in cutting out and filing newspaper clippings.

I awoke to the sound of a Niamid wrapping, as Benny swallowed a pill. Outside, the yard reverberated with dog yaps and children's voices, and the clack of volley balls striking a bat. As I was leaving, Benny jauntily accompanied me to the front door and flung it open, saying,

'Don't think you're the only one. I'll admit you're the first since I moved here. After all, the apartment isn't quite decorated yet. The other chicks haven't got on to the new number, as yet.' He laid a hand on my shoulder in a gesture of benediction. 'Let's say you've christened the apartment. Call me later kiddo.'

It was an odd farewell. I accepted the statement as an indication that Benny wished to withdraw from any kind of commitment. Finally, I succumbed to the advice of friends who were habituated to hearing of my nervous itches and insomnia. Back in my cramped one-room apartment on 54th Street, I took a shower, washed my face and pinned back my long brown hair. I changed into a sleeveless black silk dress. At an office in a pretty house in the seventies the first task was to unlock the premises, prepare hot water for coffee, and generally air the place before my employers, a Jewish businessman from Brooklyn and his rich mistress, roamed in round eleven. This morning the boss had beaten me to it.

'Come in, Jane,' he called from his room with its long windows opening out to a garden overgrown with weeds, over which sprawled deckchairs in the shade of a paradise tree. Throughout the summer days fag voices rang out from an adjoining antiquaire, every sentence punctuated with 'Ma belle' this or 'Ma belle' that.

'You look tired. Would you like me to massage your back?' The boss had tried this on me before—his large black orbs rolled in my direction. He was persuasive and I knew it. Once I was seated in the one comfortable chair, to my relief the front door slammed and his mistress entered; she was wearing pearls and a mink tippet. As I laid down the coffee cup, from her expression I could see she guessed something had been going on.

Benny haunted me all day, but I did not call. Three days passed before one evening he telephoned. He sounded peevish, but it did not prevent the usual flow. Would I care to go to a movie? I told him I had had such a busy day. How about going round for a drink? I was too exhausted to move. In that case he would come and fetch me. This was progress. He suggested coming immediately, as if he could not wait to see me. I was in bed already. Ten minutes passed before Benny swayed into the apartment in his old raincoat. He lolled on the couch with his legs splayed.

'I dreamt about you last night,' I told him.

'I'm flattered,' said Benny, and looked it.

'Why don't you take off your old raincoat?'

He glanced up sharply, 'I haven't come round for that.' But he did remove his clothes and get in the bed. He was nervous and had risen and dressed in no time. I accused him of coming round and wasting my time, and told him to beat it. Benny regarded me as if of all his women this was the biggest bitch yet. He buttoned up and the door slammed without another word being said. I was left to fume on my own. Five days passed and silence. I saw Benny reflected in every tough little man with swaying hips on the kerb. Necessity drove me to telephone.

'Thank you for calling.' Benny sounded pleased, 'I've missed you, but I would never have called again.' We arranged a meeting at once. When I apologized for my previous behaviour, he said,

'You seem to forget I've had six wives, two children, both girls, and a MOM, not to mention the many mistresses. There's nothing you can teach me about women.' We left it at that.

From then a routine was established. I was going back to Benny at the end of each day. On the occasion that friends came to my apartment for a drink while I changed some clothing, the telephone would ring; it was Benny; he would talk away, even though I stated I was not alone. Everyone was curious to see with whom I spent the evenings; but I had a sneaking suspicion Benny was a bore, although I would never be quite certain until I felt I had him—i.e. that my power over him was greater than his over me, so he remained a remote figure designated by friends as 'Total Recall'. During the day Benny telephoned the office. If I happened to be out of the room, to my annoyance he would have a long conversation with the other secretary. When a friend of his died, for days Benny went on describing each detail of the funeral; his calls always came through as the boss was entering our poke-hole and he would give me a quizzical look. My co-worker remarked: That Benny certainly seems interested, I wouldn't be surprised if we didn't hear wedding bells soon. At lunchtime we would hoist our hamburgers into the garden, sit in the deckchairs and joke about it.

I cared a good deal about eating. I liked to cook a good dinner and eat it, preferably with another person, seated at a table. Often it was depressing to get back to the troglodyte cave and find Benny in his plastic slippers, bent over the sink as he ate some scrap just dragged from the ice-box. Many times I stressed how I could stomach a heavy protein evening meal, but the deep freeze remained crammed with steaks. One hot evening, in his shorts, Benny said,

'You know, I like you. And I like having you here. I bought you some fish today.' This was progress all right. He extracted from the ice-box a carton marked Frozen Lobster Tails. I did not betray disappointment other than to remark,

'I would have preferred something fresh, you know.' Benny was doing his best. I heated the lobster tails with some butter, onion and tabasco to give the dish a little flavour. Benny did not share it. He chose to use up a cold end of T-bone steak; for another thing, he had an unshakable conviction onion brought on indigestion.

Despite an absence of mutual interests, we managed to get along, though.

Each of us carted a plate to the main room and stood eating before the television screen while Benny pontificated,

'There are only three ways of cooking . . . broiling, frying and steaming . . . etc.' To get him off a subject about which I considered he knew nothing, I said,

'I'm going to a lecture at the Whitney tomorrow,' which was Saturday.

His cool grey eyes were baleful. 'How can you possibly enjoy music or painting without understanding the rudiments? Can you describe the process of etching, for instance? It's affected to want to sit in a row of blue-haired broads listening to some fag hold forth on Degas.' In Benny's opinion a lot more could be learnt in the cavern. It was the Choc Full o' Nuts ad. that finally drove me to the bedroom.

I kicked off my patent shoes, hauled up my skirt and lay barelegged on the bed surrounded by *Nugget* and *Life* magazines.

Behind the bed was a grey silk bed back, and on either side of the bed on orange lacquer trays that Benny claimed he had painted were black bakelite lamps with black hoods, each surmounted by a black tit switch. A cardboard crate alongside the bed supported a torch, a box of Kleenex, Niamid pills and amyl nitrites that Benny liked me to crack and hold to his nostril while lovemaking, so that the floor in the morning would be littered with plaintive discarded phials, and a faint chloral odour still clung to the pillow.

A tallboy stood in the centre of the room, with bundles of undarned socks wedged between index boxes on the shelves. There were two cherry plastic chairs, on one was a fan and over the other there rested a black leather belt. Propped against the walls were gilt-framed portraits of reclining women exposing their armpits. The Venetian blinds were always down; it was impossible to tell the time of day. When there was a blue sky and the sun was shining, cracks of light filtered through and revealed the dust on the floorboards. I was contemplating this when the door burst open and Benny stood naked in the passageway.

'What are you doing in here all alone?' he hissed, as if he had caught me at something surreptitious. 'My God! You're untidy. You do it deliberately, to demonstrate your contempt.' That sounded the crankiest statement yet, considering the chaos of the room. Benny gave his gums some vigorous treatment with the dental floss and, waving his short, muscular arms, said,

'I suppose you don't know what it's like to have a friend for a lover.' I could not guess what this was leading to. A pause followed.

'The boss made another pass today.'

'I'm not a jealous man. Whatever your relations with other men, I don't want to hear about them, because it's none of my business. I'm just not a jealous man,' and he quivered. I was embarrassed and concentrated on his chest.

'Aren't you losing some weight?'

'I don't think I've changed much. After all, I'm a young man yet. Only fifty-three. And I don't want to be tied to anyone.' Benny patted his balding head and drew a photograph from the tallboy.

'After all, these were taken ten years ago. I don't think I've changed much.' Beside a row of granite-faced businessmen at a convention banquet, Benny stood pale and handsome, the cupid's bows were prominent. It was alarming to detect the change that he failed to. I watched Benny get in the bed, his holder gripped between his teeth. 'After all, I'm still young. Only fifty-three. . . . Feel. . . .' He placed my hand on his bare rump. My fingers contacted a long strip of band aid. 'What do you think that is? . . . To please you, today I went to the hospital and got a shot of hormones. What's so funny about that?' Benny concluded. I was laughing. He reached to the chair, grabbed the black belt and straddled my back with such speed I did not have a chance to struggle. He ceased beating me and sighed,

'That's relieved some tension.' Feeling for my hand, he said, 'Come here,' and cocked his head at an angle to appraise me. 'I'm thinking how attractive you are. And how much I like you.' Benny never exhibited affection. He would make a remark like, 'Since we are available to each other,' never 'Since we are attached to each other.' 'How are you doing, kiddo?' was the peak of commitment. 'I like you' must have sounded equivalent to a proposal. He looked scared and quickly added,

'I love women. Don't think you're the only one. Several women have roused me since I've known you. They don't have to be pretty, what's more.' Whereupon I voiced an opinion that enraged him more than before.

'Who are you to say so?' Benny blazed. 'The church? I have a good friend who's an analyst. You two should get together. He specializes in a certain type of operation that would be very beneficial to you. I'd see to it he did you for nothing.' Benny turned to the far edge of the bed and lapsed into a sodden sleep.

In the morning I did not say anything as I was leaving. Benny glanced up from his stool as I passed and waited for me to speak. Running, he followed me from the apartment. I felt him watch me hurry through the main hall, as he called out.

'When shall I see you again?'

With great firmness I stayed away three days. At our next meeting, standing against the sink in his shorts and slippers, Benny said,

'I missed you. I got you a present.' He reached into a store cupboard and handed me a plastic bag containing three pairs of Hi G nylon tricot sanitary panties. Moisture proof crotch. Packed under ultra violet ray. Germ free process.

'I observed them in a drugstore today. I think every dame should wear those.' Benny was attentive all the evening, swinging back and forth to the kitchen to fill my glass with ice cubes and whisky or bare kneed on the bedroom floor as he cleaned my leather skirt with Fuller's Earth.

Now of an evening as I glanced up from a magazine, Benny who was sitting opposite on the swivel stool, immersed in a newspaper, would self-consciously yawn. He would toddle to bed earlier than usual and rise in the morning more briskly. If my eyes were already open, with a funny half-smiling questioning expression, Benny would say,

'Gee! I've so much work on hand,' and catapult from the bed, to return a short while later and place a coffee cup on the lacquer tray, as he gave a bright exclamatory, 'Here we go!' supposedly to goad me to work.

I agreed to see the analyst. After all, there was no harm in having free treatment. Benny arranged for us to contact in his apartment. I must arrive on time, he said, his friend was a busy man. Benny let me in, but he did not stay, he swayed off an an errand, 'To get the groceries,' he said.

'Do you smell burning?' I asked, opening the door to the analyst. I had mislaid a cigarette and was seeking the burning fag end.

The analyst was a big gentle man, ginger in colouring, with a short bristly moustache. He answered in a soft southern drawl and humming, followed me insect-fashion round the apartment, an almost audible lull seemed to attach to each movement, as he stopped at this or that, to pick up a book or put it back—reminding me of a fly as it pauses to clean its wings on a windowpane. There was nothing weighted about his silence, it was soothing contrasted to Benny who recently had struck me as being on the verge of an hysterical scene.

After some vague conversation we sat on the couch. The analyst laid a hand on my forehead and told me to say whatever came in my head. Nothing did.

'That's no good. Relax and concentrate,' he said. For minutes we sustained this immobility, with his hand on my brow. At last I had a vision of matches.

'What do you want to do with them?'

'Strike,' I told him.

'Combined with mislaying a cigarette, this indicates an irrepressible urge to burn up poor Benny's apartment. The newspapers are a provocation.' He was grave. Benny's lifetime work eliminated. To envisage it made me laugh. The analyst was serious. Nothing further came of the meeting and another was arranged a week ahead.

The next occasion he administered a small blue pill, 'To liberate my aggression,' so he said. Benny chose to remain in the apartment and witness the reaction. To fill in time he did housework, donned orange rubber gloves and rushed round the room with a vacuum cleaner. Each time he reappeared clutching a new suctioning apparatus, in my drugged state it took the form of a sexual organ, anything circular assumed the shape of a giant maternal breast. In the bathroom the numerous sprays and dryers looked obscene, and in the room where we sat the elongated lamps with their black tit switches had a dual function. I was very elated.

'Do stop running round like a petrified rat,' I kept calling to Benny. They'd regard me with intense expectancy, as if hoping to see some violence. As the drug wore off the floating objects in the room gradually fell back in place like a completed jig saw puzzle.

There remained just Benny back on the swivel stool with a cuffed expression on his face.

The analyst now occupied my thoughts. Ginger-haired and humming he dogged me on every street car I took. I would telephone at all hours, if he refused to see me, as a last resort I'd call Benny.

Untidiness became pathological, and compulsive unreliability an ailment. I would arrive late for every appointment. Benny barely had time to file his newspaper clippings he'd be so occupied cleaning the mess I created. I would disappear for days and turn up without an explanation. Benny ceased calling the office or taking hormones. On the surface he still had control of the situation.

'You certainly like to make men spin,' he remarked once, after I had arrived two hours late and then decided to go home. One evening he entered the room and found me playfully setting light to the television screen. 'Nutty as a fruit cake,' was his verdict.

The next time I called, Benny flatly refused to see me.

'This afternoon I nearly poked out an eye on the Teevee antennae,' he related, as if it were my doing. 'I think I'll take things easy for a bit.'

A month passed. I was still having treatment. I missed Benny. He had remained adamant, responding monosyllabically each time I spoke to him.

One evening I announced I was about to call on him to gather the summer clothes left in the closet. It was only an excuse to see Benny.

The door was opened, zombie-fashion, by an unshaven Benny whose hair shot out in wisps, and although it was six in the evening he was still decked in a seersucker dressing-gown. He held his head slightly averted as if repelled by my presence. There was no conversation. He sat waiting for me to remove myself. Alone I entered the bedroom; my clothes were heaped in a dust mound beside the tallboy; face creams had been scooped from their jars and smeared on the dresses over which were stubbed out filter tips; the smell of grease and ashes was sickening. Benny had had some kind of squalid tantrum.

A month or so later I and the analyst who was wearing a deerstalker, tweed jacket and prophylactic overshoes, were sitting in a drugstore on the last two vacant stools. By now I knew his wardrobe consisted almost entirely of herring-bone. It was winter, muffled men with plastic ear pieces like headphones kept entering and stamping their boots free of snow which immediately thawed and ran in rivulets round the base of each bar stool. Everyone was ordering coffee and bacon and egg sandwiches. The analyst related that Benny, of his own volition, had entered a psychiatric ward in a New Jersey clinic.

We were on our way to the country, melled in the rat race of weekenders fleeing Manhattan, driving past chains of supermarkets and rotting scrap metal dumps. Tinselled streamers fluttered across the fill-up stations. Christmas was approaching. I was studying the billboards. Posters help breed freedom of choice. Your dog needs meat—Alpho meat chunks. No litter 50 dollars fine. . . .

'Poor old Benny. A reformed alcoholic. Frittered all his money on women. A few years back he had a stroke and the doctors predicted that if he lived it up again, it would be the end of Benny. Now he can't touch the family fortune. His mother gives him an allowance. Now and then he gets depressive, feels the need to be cosseted and veers toward the nearest clinic. Poor old Benny . . .' said the analyst who was not a day under sixty.

'Why all those gadgets and machines? The telephone never rang anyway.'

'Firms do sometimes get on to Benny for data. He provides it at a very low rate. He started off very brilliantly.' The analyst remained silent.

'And why did the marriages collapse?'

'Three wives he sent to me for treatment. The first complained he awoke each morning with the words, I've got to be somebody! Will I ever make it! Another was haunted by his nightmares. How Benny would shriek in his sleep, but awoke with some gallant dead-pan joke. Finally, he was always loaded.'

We drove into some Honeymoon Hamlets. A registered nurse was standing at the entrance and over the portal was written, Where Friend Meets Friend. Holly wreaths attached with red ribbons and bells dripped from the door knobs. We settled in.

'Are you all right, darling?' said the analyst. Humming, he disappeared into a closet and modestly removed his herringbone. 'I think I'll take a good hot bath,' sounded like an apology.

Honeymoon Hamlet was run by Quakers. There was no bar, no drink could be sent upstairs or served in the dining-room where waitresses in white sneakers and aprons administered set course meals. 'I think I'll pass up on dinner,' said the analyst.

In a corner of the grounds secluded amongst the conifers was a liquor store and we bought Scotch and two small flagons of Moussec. Ice was sent up to the twin-bedded room. I drank and read and gazed out at the chipmunks swinging from the conifers while the analyst went for a stroll.

That night, feeling in some way responsible, I remarked on the dour mood he was in. Mulling over what I said, in order to give a reasonable explanation, he replied,

'It made me think of my wife today as we drove through those dogwood trees. She lives in a nearby asylum.'

It is expected that Benny will be out soon, but I don't think about him so much these days, as the analyst has me hooked.

Sour Grapes

'I'm such a shit,' he repeated, his face was radiant. An eager beagle with a brief case under one arm, he stood expectantly waiting to be let out.

'You think admitting it makes it better?' I sounded censorious, and unlatched the door. Jubilantly hitching up his pinstripe, he said,

'I know all about that kind of argument.' Sprinting past, his face glowing anew, he hustled along the grubby dun walls of the corridor and down the five flights of slum block. At the bottom, he called, 'See you soon, kiddo.'

I had never thought of Ben Gold as a shit. It was a strong word for Ben, and not his habitual tone. As if to refute the statement, slipped beneath an Elizabeth David cook book on the dresser was another cheque. I was touched. Laughingly, I'd told him it made me feel a kind of Fanny Hill. Ben, fleeing even faster along the hallway, had emitted his nervous manic bray, and called, 'Get yourself a little blouse or something, kiddo.' Another time he'd say, 'Buy some chow, baby.'

Lately, though, Ben's mind seemed to be taken up with more pressing matters than tact. Payments were handed across like tacit guilt tokens. Not that Ben had need to feel guilt. Perhaps only because as his buddies claimed, Ben was such a sweet fellow.

My last job, two years back, had been painting papier maché cats in Mexican reds and greens for Serendipity. Since then, applying as an illustrator, I had covered the publishing houses. 'Degrees?' they asked. My portfolio of drawings was not even opened.

Now that I had given up looking for work altogether, I had taken on a new lease of life. I could not understand why on each occasion we met, friends went on asking, 'Found a job yet?' By now they should have become as discouraged as I had. Luckily, I had warm-hearted friends who, when going to Europe or Florida, called me in for company to witness their packing. I was given any delectable scraps that might have remained rotting in the ice-box for weeks; violent lipsticks; and discarded clothing that would otherwise be destined for the Salvation Army in Harlem. Wherever I went I took a Mexican basket ready to scoop old magazines into, once everyone else had perused them. It made people feel good, and fostered an illusion that they weren't wasteful. Essentials like soap and light bulbs often got swept into my basket off Lamston's counter during a crowded luncheon hour.

Ben had been promoted Managing Editor of a publishing house. He'd incorporated his needy pals into the firm on some basis or other when I would have been happy to get taken on as a cleaning woman. I was prepared to do almost anything to tide me over.

Once ensconced in his new job, Ben's glossy black olive eyes became more euphorically defiant. Contempt had set in, I decided. Obsessed with Ben's inconsistency I pumped anyone who had an inkling into his character. Ben was an adolescent prodigy. He'd graduated at fourteen, and already been analysed at sixteen. Everyone admiringly agreed Ben was clever and conscientious, and had a memory that was a phenomenon. He was curious and knowing on every serious topic, and the first recipient of any news or gossip. He had to be up-to-date or else he felt he was slipping. A dependable slogger, he never indulged in flashes of wit or brilliance. Ben loved to help people. Across a crowded room his voice would vibrate, 'I can lay it on for you, kiddo.' and he did. He was devoted to his friends. They formed a fashionable elite. Those he had met in Europe were almost certain to have a trace of royalty in their background. Girls proud to be selected because of the kudos, were handed from one member to the other and shed like seasonal membranes. Ben assembled the pieces. He treated women as pals. Those of his special choice always met with the elite's approval. He was attractive to women, bringing out their maternal feelings. At parties when wives fondled the boyish sleek head, it made Ben uneasy, especially if their husbands were looking on, he ducked, and to his escort's relief, as he may have ignored her all evening, it being draggy to appear saddled with someone, he sidled up, and said, 'Time to go home, baby.'

Ben was seldom with the same girl for long. In the initial stage he nestled on a sofa about to lay his head on her bosom as though paying court to Aphrodite. Men who'd shared the same girls reporting that as far as they gathered once Ben was lured into a bedroom nothing much ensued bar a few pecks on the cheek; mostly the girls resented being dropped off on the kerb while Ben sprang smartly back into the cab, calling, 'A lot of work on hand, kiddo.'

'But then you ought to know,' they concluded. I never let on my experience. So I hinted that Ben lacked something.

Reminded of his attributes I warmed to Ben, mostly I loved his encyclopediac mind. Anything to do with the common market or a pending election and pronto Ben supplied the information, even if I did forget it seconds later.

I first got to know Ben after a winter in Jamaica. I called to report on the interesting introductions he had provided. That night we went to Romeo and Juliet; it was the one time we'd been alone together. Back at my louche hotel with no prompting Ben stayed overnight. Every day Ben returned and clasped me in a bear's hug. For a month we held hands and necked on sofas, in corridors and in cabs, oblivious of the drivers. To vary the procedure Ben lifted me off my feet, I was lithe and easy to wield, and swung me above his head as you would rock a child, so that I felt like making delighted gurgles I was so happy to sense the pleasure Ben got from being a strong amorous male. Particularly when after six weeks he finally made it.

Our first party I hardly knew anyone. I lacked Ben's enthusiasm, but found his clan a decent lot. A small girl with grey eyes and a bob I stood slightly apart dressed in tight black leather like one of the boys from the sado-masochist club. My main claim to fame was having been one of Kennedy's girls. A glass in one hand and a cigarillo in the other I tried to be swinging. If I cracked a joke Ben supplied a loyal embarrassed guffaw. After the party, Ben exclaimed, 'My God! Some silly girl gave me her key. Why should she do that! I'd better take it to her.' Two hours passed. I thought that was the last of him, but Ben came panting back.

Summer came. The city was abandoned. A rich buddy, Jack, lent Ben his apartment overlooking Central Park. I moved in. Between job-hunting I kept house.

It seemed to irk Ben to spend an evening a deux or to take interest in a dinner. Unless there was a buddy around or a party immediately he was home he brought out work. Ben was seldom satisfied with an author. If the content was good the style was poor. Ben was a stickler for detail, he distrusted intuitive assessments. Between munches beside the sink he might rewrite a whole book. If I commented on his assiduity, Ben said, 'The President's going to read this one and it's got to be good.'

Ben would help me with the job tests dished out by fashion magazines. Ben assured me I had talent. 'Plod on, baby,' he'd say, completing my illustration while I averted my gaze from Central Park and made an encouraging comment over his broad shoulder. He was as scrupulous over my job tests as over his own work.

Before his parents visited us, I said, 'Won't they be surprised to see me here?'

'They're swinging people,' said Ben, 'Tremendously up on everything. They'll be pleased I'm with a girl for once. Unmarried, they see me as the misfit of the family.' The parents conformed to a not uncommon pattern, a domineering mother with a gentle deflated husband. Now retired they kept a duck farm. In a conscious effort to convey zeal in their company Ben retained an on-the-ball smirk. It was a strain. I was glad to see them go.

After six weeks Ben's sprints from the bed grew more precipitate. I jeered about him to friends and made sneering insinuations.

The second month Ben complained of the increase of work in the office, and how he would have to stay late. He stayed later and later. Finally, he spent whole nights there, or so he told me. He returned at dawn for a short nap, coffee and pep pills.

It irked Ben to come home and find me wandering round in a blue kaftan with baleful swollen kohl-rimmed eyes.

'What is it? baby.' Ben was tender and solicitous. 'Have I hurt you? What is it?' Ben gathered up the kohl sticks, bobby pins, and wet wads of cotton and frowningly swept them into old shaving boxes.

One afternoon I was bent over a job test in my kaftan surrounded by make-up when a call came from a hospital. Ben had been rushed there in an ambulance. I called every day. It seemed Ben had had a heart attack. The nurses said he was doing as well as could be expected.

The end of summer Jack returned from Europe. With Ben's blessing, it was hinted, a liaison blossomed between buddy, Jack, and me; it was small consolation and died the usual death with little regret either side. I found a place of my own and moved out.

Ben was due to leave the hospital and I received a summons. Would I hurry round with a suitcase staunch enough for the hoard of books acquired during his internment. Two pretty girls were already there loading up with paperbacks.

In slippers and a sagging suit Ben followed our suitcases into the elevator. It was the evening rush hour. Ben hailed a passing trash truck; it was the kind of impulse his friends admired so. We clamboured in. The girls dropped off, he took me on to buddy, Terry's for the one night prior to his recuperation in Florida where sojourns had been arranged for Ben by buddies whose mothers had winter residences in Palm Beach.

Parties given in Terry's apartment with its Picassos and Buffets and beautiful vista of the Hudson, of the trawlers and the city reflected on the water at night, were the most daring in Manhattan; anything from a chic Jackie gathering to an orgy or a blue film might be on. Ben's first night out was no exception. Pot was produced. From the bed Ben rolled and twisted each cigarette. Everyone smoked squatting, drank and chatted of the latest books with snippets about the authors provided by Ben who had been fed gossip, computer-fashion, in the hospital. Ben always got left with the roach. He happily rolled another and passed it on until the company decided he was ashen.

The guests gone, Ben wanted to hear every intimate detail of my affair with buddy, Jack, when all I wanted was to describe my new apartment over the Fabulous Fakes Antiques. I had to relate everything twice. Instead of saying, Goodnight, kiddo, sleep well, and switching his back, Ben clasped me in a bear's hug all night.

The two girls arrived with a hire car laid on by Jack to escort the invalid to the airport. Ben kissed me three times, and came back and kissed me a fourth before bolting on to the runway. I was very sorry to see Ben go.

I received an express letter to say how passionate Ben felt, and how he wished I were there. I answered in a similar vein. Ben wrote two more love letters to say he was in a hot fantasy thinking about me, working hard, had not much time for buddies, and felt lonely . . . the mornings are dewey here and the nights would be lovelier if you were moving through them . . . Yours ever, Ben. They were followed by two months' silence.

I eagerly awaited Ben's return. He never called when he got back, instead he sent me two tickets for the Sadler's Wells ballet.

The next time we met, I had returned from Connecticut and Ben had formed a publishing house of his own. He still needed capital, and was chasing about in search of investors. He was avidly interested to hear whom I'd been seeing. Anything I told him he already knew. 'And how have you been?' I asked, 'Still busy with your pencil?' Ben looked startled. He thought I was getting at him. 'Oh! Churning away with worry. Everywhere I go second-raters whom I rather like and want me to commission books, I'm obliged to put them off so I rather not see a lot of them, the subject of my lack of confidence in them lies between us unspoken. I see quite enough of my immediate colleagues during the day and whatever their other virtues one's not really drawn to them as pals and so the orbit narrows . . . and the worries mount . . .'

'Poor baby!' I thought Ben improved with confidence, and merely wanted to reach out a tiny hand and smoothe the sleek black hair. 'And how's Harriet?' I asked. My closest friend in New York whom Ben tolerated as a successful narcissistic clothes horse.

'She called me several times a few months ago. I took her to a few parties. A Latin American snapped her up. By then I considered I'd done my bit.'

Solemn-faced Ben delivered what sounded like a rehearsed utterance, 'I've thought about you a lot. Sometimes I feel badly at the way I carry on. There's some kind of fate attached to you, baby, that I'm fighting all the time. How are things in the job line?'

We resumed all the same. Ben came back to the apartment over Fabulous Fakes. He worked late and might turn up at any hour of the night. I went on doing children's illustrations, maybe one day someone would take a shine to them. Or I painted the view of the blue sky, the teevee poles, air conditioners and drain pipes.

The sixth week, after a hurried breakfast, facing the mirror, Ben said, 'I'm getting fat, baby.'

'It's the sedentary life you lead.'

'Never any time for exercise. I miss not having a knock up or swim. There I go wailing again. Always sorry for myself.' Ben had not time for a shower. He rushed into the kitchen for his brief case. 'So much work, kiddo. It's terrible this treadmill I've got myself on to . . . nothing but work work work. I'll be sleeping in the office tonight.'

'Well, call me later.'

Ben glared, 'Call you?'

'We needn't talk for long.'

'Listen, kiddo,' Ben paused, choosing his words to avoid causing pain, 'You've always said you like honesty. You know what's the matter with me? I don't go for fidelity.'

'You mean there's someone else?'

'Not exactly,' Ben paused, 'not exactly,' and added tactfully, 'but I might. I expect you to do the same. I'm a shit, you see.'

I was stunned. If any man were capable of fidelity I'd have thought Ben had it in him. Perhaps the clan were against it . . . en principe.

His footsteps pounded down the stairs. 'Kiddo! Kiddo!' echoed along the dun walls on a plaintive note of panic similar to the bleat of 'Ma' from the juveniles each time they returned from school and banged on the door of the apartment opposite.

It was then I hurried the last cheque to the hardware store now familiar with Ben's signature. That was the end of him. Weeks went by. I confess I was baffled. Perhaps by then as Ben had said of Harriet, 'he considered he'd done his bit.' But to prefer to sleep on a mattress spread on a raggy carpet of a book-congested room when he could have been in my Beauty Rest and be brought coffee and fruit juice for breakfast was more than I could comprehend.

The shaving cream and shirts given to the super who despatched the tenants' gifts home to Ireland, and Moon of Alabama on my mind, for weeks I went on humming, we've lost our good old Papa . . . got to have dollars . . . oh you know why . . . and brooded where the 'next pretty boy' and 'little dollar' were coming from.

One day I called Ben. He sounded harassed. That evening I met him in his disorderly apartment with the socks and sneakers strewn about. Nervously watching me sort his shirts, Ben laughed 'Quite something, isn't it? You don't look too good. I have an account with a travel agent. Just charge any ticket to me. And forward any pressing bills.' Ben gave me a quizzing look. I was more peaked than usual. 'Don't grieve. Don't grieve.' He referred to Kennedy's death. 'It's far worse for me. The new President's not going to take an interest in anything I bring out.' Ben frowned into the distance, as if his goal were receding.

We made our way to Jack's wedding reception. There were speeches.

A large buffet. Two bands. Harriet joined our table. She congratulated Jack. Taking me aside, she said,

'What's up with Ben? Dines me every night. Drops me home, and says, Call you, kiddo.'

Moodily inclined toward Harriet, his head swaying over her bodice, at midnight Ben said to me,

'It's terrible this treadmill I'm on. Like me to see you home?'

'Everyone's on some kind of treadmill.'

'Are you?' Ben's mouth pursed. 'Anyone offered you a job?'

'Jack's made a good marriage, hasn't he?'

Ben looked Panicky. Without trying to conceal the insouciant manner of a man with appointments on his mind Ben put me into a cab, and ducked back under the awning.

The next day I went to the little tailor embalmed in a hole in the wall. His lined face was beaming. 'Very good,' He held up the alteration. 'I start tailoring as a baby.'

'How long have you been in America?'

'Since the war. The Germans put me in eight camps. I show you something,' he pulled up his sleeve, 'The number they give me at Auschwitz.' I gazed morbidly at the tiny blue tatoos on his forearm. The tailor was smiling. 'It's been lucky to me ever since. The luck that number's brought me! Only last week I won fifty dollars gambling on it.'

Three idlers seated on stools in the back laughed with him.

'Eight camps,' they intoned, 'You know why? So you don't get familiar with the guards. That's what they were avoiding.' They offered me coffee. 'Stay for a chat,' one said.

'Come back and I'll do you a new suit,' said the tailor.

I felt a different person walking with my repaired skirt to the Guggenheim. The Brancusi and Giacommeti drawings made me feel even better. Leaving the Museum I walked along Central Park. On the opposite side in the Fifties I saw Ben gazing into buddy, Jonathan's, blue

blue eyes as into a clear blue sky on a summer day. No longer young, Jonathan still carried himself like an Eton boy; he had narrow shoulders, slender hips and a skip. They halted at the box office of a movie house. 'Let me, old boy.' Ben was saying. He inclined toward Jonathan who laid an affectionate hand on his arm as if to arrest Ben's insistent attempt to pay. I had never seen Ben so carefree, like a child playing truant. I felt intrusive. Without a backward glance I turned the bend.

Round buffet tables everywhere I saw Ben escorting Harriet who gazed admiringly up at him. Ben had moved into her house with a suitcase. She had never been so involved, she said. She was taking him to Europe in the summer.

Harriet went to Europe. Ben went from success to success. Friends only hoped he'd settle before his health gave out.

I was travelling about. Back in New York I saw Ben leaping distractedly in and out of a hired Rolls, rushing into the Colony, the Pavilion, and the Four Seasons.

Always absorbed in some new flourishing scheme he had scant leisure to spare. Anxious to be helpful and likeable, Ben went on promising people better jobs and contacts. It would have been impossible to placate everyone! Men began to speak ill as their wives took increasing interest in Ben bent over yet another glamorous bosom.

At the last party he appeared paler, plumper and blooming. I told him I was cashing in on Pop. That I bought up doorknobs on credit from the hardware and painted them with faces in alphabetical forms. I was exhibiting in Museums in the Mid West. It wasn't lucrative, but it kept me going.

'Good for you, baby, Good for you. Keep it up.' His eyes unglossed. Returning his focus on the door he remarked that at last I seemed to have gauged the tempo of the city, and allotted me more of his time than usual.

Finally, sighing dolefully, he said, 'So lonely, baby. I lead such a lonely life.' The laugh had a desperate ring.

'I hear you're marrying a Spence-Vanferfeller.'
Ben brightened. 'Who knows! Who knows!' The pursed sphincter smirk was from embarrassment. I reached out toward the greying English-cut head. His sultry eyes roved the company. Ducking, he said, 'Call you kiddo,' and bolted across the room.

This is the Life

An unhappy romance had driven Rosie back to California to live with her mother. The winter had been bleak without a lover. Rosie had saved up enough to take a trip. She had always wanted to see Mexico. From friends she heard that if you were careful to avoid eating fruit, meat and uncooked vegetables, and never swallowed the water even while cleaning your teeth, the visit could be an experience of a lifetime.

Rosie did not like to travel alone, still, one morning she made the decision and purchased some dysentry pills. She boarded a bus in the mountains behind San Francisco. Fields were blazing with mustard, and the roads scented with eucalyptus. Pink and white fruit blossom heralded the spring.

Driving down the coast they passed salvage dumps, scrap heaps, billboards, trailer parks and dusty orange groves. Rosie had always thought of the West coast as being beautiful. It was no compensation to be seated beside a stout man who dug into her so that she wished she had brought along knee spurs.

L.A. was smoggy and stifling. She felt claustrophobic looking out at the solid office buildings, and the endless stretches of automobiles glistening in the sun.

In San Diego the 'Safe, Reliable and Courteous' driver announced, 'Hope you enjoyed your trip, folks.' He helped everyone off the bus.

Rosie was staying over-night and placed her baggage in a locker. The terminal was packed with servicemen. Trusting owl-faced old ladies dozed over pouter chests gleaming with tinselled orchid sprays. In the cafeteria Rosie ate a 'Frank on a Bun with Spuddies' pumpkin pie and coffee. At dawn she took a bus to the border.

Rosie had been warned not to stay in Tijuana, a shanty town of immense filth, populated by pimps and whores. It was already ninety degrees as she carried a knapsack, suitcase and camera through the customs. The town of Tijuana was two miles away. A huddle of cabs awaited an influx of tourists. Rosie hailed the nearest. The cabman had salacious lips, a black moustache, and oily hair in the shape of a pudding basin. On the way into the town, he said,

'I'll give you twenty dollars for fifteen minutes.'

'I don't have the time, I'm afraid.'

'Thirty dollars for ten, then. It won't take longer.'

'I'm late for my bus as it is.'

Without demanding the fare he dropped her outside the House of Girlesque, and drove off. Rosie carried her baggage on to the bus terminal five minutes walk away. The terminal smelt of spiced garlic. No more scrubbed faces and uniformity. In bright cottons and shawls peasants sat placidly nursing bundles. Epicene tubs squatted under sombreros.

A chewing crew-cut driver stood checking the tickets. When Rosie's turn came his gum relaxed. His pocked face lit up as though this were the long lost love he'd been awaiting all his life. His teeth flashed, 'Guapa,' he murmured.

Small boys mounted the bus with packets of chiclets to sell. The driver removed his jacket and switched the radio knob. The bus drove off to a blare of cha-cha-cha. Smiling, the driver watched Rosie in the windscreen mirror. Beside the mirror was written, Cigarettes Only, next to a crucifix.

Soon they were at the top of a mountain pass. The pinnacles had niches, each on shading a blue virgin. On either side of the road were giant bolders. In the distance the road cut knife-like through a desert dotted with broom and agave. They descended on to a plateau. Dead branches straggled at an abrupt angle on which humming birds perched. Cacti stood bolt up like fingered totems. The huts were of earth and wattle sheltered by tamarisks. Washing hung from the trees and was strung across to gutless broken-down automobiles.

On the first billboard Tecate was written, Squirt followed, and Ahorre, Carta Blanca, and Pepsi-Cola. They were approaching a village. Along the blank road a motor-bike appeared. The bus driver was halted for speeding.

They drew into the bus stop to a blare of cha-cha-cha. His eye on Rosie in the mirror, the driver shouted in English, 'Fourteen minute here.' The peasants responded with fortitude. Rosie bought a bottle of Cerveza Superior, and drank it in a dusty yard in the hot sun, and watched two tailless cats scrabble over a cockroach.

Forty minutes later the bus proceeded. At dusk the bus reached Mazatlan. The pocked one took Rosie across the street and offered her some goat cheese with tortilla, and fresh oysters in chili sauce from an oyster stall. They stood on the kerb and peered at each other in the gloaming. When he spoke it was gibberish. If she spoke, he said, 'Why?' His expression was pleading.

The bus filled. A crew-cut relief driver took over. The pocked one relaxed in the seat beside Rosie. A long time he peered at her, trying to make conversation. Then his eyes closed.

The middle of the night Rosie was awakened by a bite in the lobe of her ear. His hand had unbuttoned her levis and reached the vital area. 'All mine,' he said. Rosie pushed his hand away. 'Why?' he repeated. It was too dark to see the pleading look. All around the noble peasants were sleeping. His hand plunged anew. After an hour's quiet struggle Rosie gave up. His hand remained there immovable. She covered it with a pillow.

They entered Escuinapa to a blaze of cha-cha-cha. Rosie glanced back to see if anyone had witnessed the night's scuffle. The lined faces expressed forbearance. At Escuinapa they ate. Afterwards the driver said, 'Honey. Come.' He led her into a cobbled square and kissed her leaning against the wall of the beautiful Baroque Cathedral.

The bus was sprayed. The peasants came back with bunches of pinks wrapped in old newspapers. The pocked one took over the wheel. Swaying like a pendulum as the bus rounded the mountainous hair pin bends he kept up a raucous conversation with a pretty woman in black who had boarded at Escuinapa. She rejoined with unrestrained laughter. In the crepuscular light Rosie stared angrily into the windscreen mirror and saw a pocked bat with flapping ears.

The next stop was a large railway terminal. Alone, Rosie sipped Cerveza Superior. Curled up forms in serapis lay about the platforms, beside them were baskets of strawberries. The relief driver took over. The pocked one seated himself next to Rosie. By now he had conjured up more English.

'We elope. Mekhiko City we elope. Middle of night. You come? Me single. You no? We marry. Me make much money driving. Honeymoon Acapulco. Acapulco beautiful. Swim. You take me America.' His gum shifted. He stroked his crew cut. He kept this up for an hour. Rosie began to find him endearing.

The middle of the night the bus reached Mekhiko City. The pocked one checked the tickets. Rosie ate a greasy omelette in the terminal, and accompanied him in the empty bus to park it with the others in a garage. He would not let her carry her baggage. 'Me Spanish gentleman.' He proudly showed a white patch under his watch strap on an otherwise Indian skin.

He signed the hotel register. In the bare double room he rang for Cerveza Superior and disappeared. Rosie paid for the beer when it came. Back in the room he sat in his shirt sleeves laboriously bent over a ledger book on the dressing table. Rosie took a shower. There were holes in the sheets. Rosie was asleep in no time. Next day it would be different.

In the morning he had great plans for the future. First, he must hand in his ledger at the office. After he would show her the Cathedral. Then Acapulco beautiful! His car was parked opposite.

Naked, he stood waving frenetically to a group of men in the car park. Shaking with laughter he went on waving and thumbing at Rosie beside him. 'Amigos,' he told her. He went on waving and grimacing as if enjoying a huge joke. Rosie ignored the antics and went on putting her clothes in the knapsack. They left the baggage ready to pick up later.

In the hotel restaurant they ate ham and eggs, and drank fresh pineapple juice for breakfast. They entered the car park together. Suddenly, from half-way across the tarmac a little pinched black-clad woman, ravaged with sleeplessness and rage, and hair flecked with grey, ran fleeting toward them, holding in her arms a baby. There was a loud harangue. She grabbed the pocked one. Screaming, she tugged him away. Shame-faced, he followed protesting feebly. They got into a broken down car and drove away. Rosie might as well not have been there. The amigos had witnessed the scene with equanimity. At a loss Rosie approached them to ask the way to the Cathedral. Each amigo silently turned his back. Rosie felt foolish walking back in the hot sun the way she had come five minutes ago. In the streets men stared and muttered 'Guapa'.

The rest of the morning Rosie gazed with unseeing eyes at monumental Aztec sculpture. Back in the hotel she paid for the double room and breakfast. There was no message. It was lonely in the room with the stacked baggage. She asked the way to the bus terminal.

'Very close,' said the hall porter. What's more, he could provide her with an amigo to help carry the baggage. 'A good amigo,' he stressed knowingly. She need have no fear. The amigo was staying in the hotel. At the appointed hour the porter introduced them in the lobby. The amigo turned out to be a bull-fighter. It was Sunday. The corrida was that afternoon. Dignified and silent, the bull-fighter walked beside her carrying the baggage as far as the ticket office. He said,

'Acapulco hermoso. Full but hermoso. Height of season.' He held out his card. Rosie was prepared to sleep on the beach if necessary, and told him so. He bowed and kissed her hand before leaving.

The bus departed to the drone of cha-cha-cha which quickly changed to the corrida broadcast from Mekhiko arena. Three hours the whistling crowd roared as if faenas succeeded estocadas. The noise terminated as the bus turned on to Acapulco promenade.

'Vacancy' signs loomed out of the blackness. The new motels, the hotels, the sea and the mountains were invisible. Rosie stopped at the first hotel she came to. It was empty. In the shower a giant cockroach scuttled over her toe and tried to climb the wall to escape the onrush of water.

She was awoken early by the sound of children's voices like the buzzing of thousands of insects inside her head. Her window looked on to a High School.

The streets had the aroma of a hot farmacia mixed with drainage. Along the uriniferous wall of the promenade men in sombreros sat cross-legged sewing. Picking strands of wool from the paving they were stitching bulbous floral designs on to wide straw hats and baskets that were finally displayed in the market. The beaches ran parallel to the main road. Pedestrians and cyclists lazed against the palms and gloated at the sun bathers a few feet away. It was sweltering. The sea was still and blue. The sand was pale and smoothe. In the far distance the desolate mountains were beckoning. The hotel had recommended the Caleta beach. Hermoso! It was in the opposite direction. Rosie walked another hour. The sun was in its zenith. Seen from the main road the Caleta was shaped like a new moon with launches moored off shore. A little way out to sea rose a rock with an ochre villa enfolded in palms on the top. Bordering the beach, in the throes of erection, a new building opened like a vast cement beehive. A man hacked at the pavement. Next to the beehive was a restaurant. The Bum. Bum. And a café, El Cabana.

Rosie went into the Bum Bum to change into a swimsuit. In the cloakroom a man broomed out an overflow. Her sneakers got drenched. There was the sound of cha-cha-cha, and someone practising castanets. A barrel organ played. A juke box moaned. Fresh orange juice? They had none. Pineapple juice? None either. Any fresh fruit juice? Bottled orangeade. No ice, though.

Despondent, Rosie lay on the scorching sand and pined for a glass of homogenized milk. A man approached with a guitar. A waiter ran up with the offer of another warm orangeade. Men in sombreros roamed the sands balancing trays of potted custard, elaborately embellished straw hats, souvenir ashtrays. ornamental marlins, giant coloured postcards, and sandles in plastic bags.

The sea was warm. On the surface myriads of black specks floated. They evaporated to the touch and left a smear on the hand. It looked as if not far off a sewage pipe was disgorging. Seeing Rosie in the water two sombreros rushed forward with a tripod, a Rolleiflex and a flash lamp. In spite of her protests they snapped her diving into a vortex of bobbing refuse. 'Olé,' one man said.

Back on the sand, and cooler, at any rate, Rosie listened to the Canadian and German tourists enlarging on their journey down. They made plans to combine on boat trips. Behind Rosie, under an umbrella, were a Mid-Western family of three who kept to themselves. A large white pouter-breasted mother, a father and a son in his thirties. They all wore the bulky wool straw hats of the region.

The son neared the water. 'Watch out, Al. Don't go in too far now.' 'Alright, Ma,' he said, impatiently, taking a look at the sea and quickly retracing his footsteps.

'I wanna have coconut juice,' the old lady whined, as the Bum Bum waiter came running up with the offer of an orangeade for the third time. 'I told you I wanna have coconut juice.' The waiter clambered a palm and shook a frond. A coconut landed with a dead thud on the sand. The waiter re-appeared with a machete. 'Watcha put in it?' said the old lady. 'Whisky? Gin? Anything.' The waiter volunteered helpfully.

Hatted, a camera in each lap, the family of three drank the spirited coconut juice out of straws, passing the hairy hard kernel like a loving cup. A photographer ran up with a tripod. A man arrived with some custard pots, another handed out souvenir ashtrays. Soon the trio were surrounded. They fingered the marlins, tried on the sandles, and took

their pick of the post cards. Leaning back satisfied, the son said,
'All for two dollars ! This is the life, Ma.'

The light was changing. Rosie felt lonely on the beach by herself. She took a comb from her bag; at the bottom lay the bull-fighter's card. Rosie gathered up her belongings. She walked back to the hotel. She packed her baggage and paid the bill. The porter looked surprised to see her go. In the terminal she bought a ticket and sat on a bench, waiting for the next cha-cha-cha bus to take her back to Mekhiko City.

How Much Longer?

'God! I wish I were dead. Just look at those lines.' Maggie obeyed. Perdita was reflected in the mirror naked, but for the thin gold bangles on her wrist and a giant aquamarine on her finger. Aloof and erect, with stunning grey hair, and perfectly alright breasts she was fond of exposing, long legs and boyish hips, she carried her six feet with immense poise.

Perdita had just had her teeth evened; being a photographic model, she hoped it would bring her more television commercials. It had made all the difference to her life, she said, and smiled into the mirror as proof of it. The smile of someone prepared for a camera flash. She pointed out the miniscule varicose vein on the thigh that the doctor could do nothing with but worsen. Instead, she said, she was going to have the bags removed from under her wide apart eyes.

'You're crazy. You don't have any,' said Maggie, who feared that at any moment Perdita was going to bring out some scissors. Perdita liked her friends to be as well turned out as herself. This caused continual friction between them. 'You could be quite an attractive woman if you took more care of yourself.' Perdita was always saying. To avoid a scene Maggie resignedly gave in when Perdita clipped off her hair, making her face look like a balloon, or insisted she use a certain shade of lipstick, telling her not to shape her mouth into a Jean Harlow bow.

Maggie first met her in Rome just after the war when Perdita had fled Paris, leaving a French Count after six months of marriage. Everyone knew of Perdita in Rome. She had bit parts in films, and looked so striking dressed elegantly in the latest Pucci model with a scarf to blend; being driven round in an open Mercedes by the handsome latin with whom she was living.

Perdita differed from the common rut of American women with their provincial clothes, and refreshingly outgoing manner. She gave the impression she had to put herself out to be nice to people.

As a child she'd been obsessed by her nose; she thought she looked like a hawk. Maggie ran into her again after Perdita had suffered four nose operations. She was finally getting it righted by a famous plastic surgeon in London. She then married a handsome Englishman. Three months later she left him. She returned to the States after an absence of fifteen years, and here Maggie caught up with her again.

'God!' Perdita repeated into the mirror, 'How much longer must one keep it up. A few more years and I'm going to swim out to sea and never come back.'

The temperature was nintey-three and humid. The house was steaming. It had been a ritual throughout the summer, when neither had been invited away for the weekend, for them to get together and console each other on Maggie's rooftop. Perdita would arrive at noon on Saturday with an over-night bag. Both had an avid need to roast their bodies. Though their skin had lost some elasticity, each retained the shape she'd had in a youthful heyday.

Wearing swimsuits, they carried the chaises longues up the stairs and laid them out on the scorching green asphalt. Every half-hour they went down into the steaming apartment, showered off the sweat, and applied tan lotion. Maggie had spent so much of her life in the sun she had reached a state of immunity; she could lie in it every day without getting browner, all that ever happened was her hair got brassy.

The five T.V. poles, the other tenant's washing hanging on the line above their heads, the smuts from the myriads of tiny black incinerator funnels on the adjoining roofs, and the new skyscraper buildings nearing completion in the distance with Now Renting plastered across, prompted Maggie to say,

'We should get some sleeping bags for up here.'

'Old sleeping bags, that's us.' Perdita laughed, in better spirits than she had been for years. She had brought round a small pot of caviar and some Rhine wine to celebrate her new love affair. She watched Maggie in the billowy black satin swimsuit she had given her, wearing it minus its belt, of course. Maggie was setting down the bench she had carried up for them to eat off.

It amazed and amused Perdita the way Maggie looked with her brassy hair, no eyebrows and spiky lashes, and yet still managed to be attractive to men.

She liked to hear of Maggie's experiences. Not that she approved of Maggie's choice; they were usually ugly, old or midgets. Perdita could not walk down a street with anyone conspicuously shorter. She had to be seen with someone young and cute-looking. And since a month she had been. A queer friend had produced him.

After a succession of fleeting adventures, each one leaving Perdita in a state of trauma, so that for months after she planned how to get her own back on the person who had failed her, Perdita was really in love. She was so anxious to make this work, she said, in spite of her death wish, she was prepared to make every compromise.

'I'd rather die than have to spend the rest of my life living alone.'

'Is Pete away this weekend?'

'He's visiting his parents in Chicago. Next week he's taking me to meet them. I said your mother won't be pleased to see me. Apparently, she's so afraid he's going to be homosexual, she's relieved to see him with any woman.'

'Has he found any work?'

'I got him a job with a photographer. He hates it, the regular hours, and the boredom. The trouble is he thinks he's no good at anything. If it hadn't been for me he was going back to that bar in Torremolinos.'

Maggie laid out the glasses and the Rhine wine. They ate the caviar on buttered toast with chopped raw onion and lemon, and agreed how good it was. Perdita was appreciative when Maggie cooked something delicious, she was more finicky than Maggie whose appetite was bestial.

Driven together a lot of the time from force of circumstance, their one common interest was food.

Maggie appeared through the roof hatch with a chicken in aspic and tarragon.

'Pete's on the blower.'

'Did you say I was here? I don't want him to think I never have anything better to do.'

When Perdita came back to the roof, she said, 'Pete's quarrelled with his mother. He wanted to come round. I said I had a date. That he could pick me up here at six.' Perdita had her desperate look.

She rushed down the stairs followed by Maggie with the dishes. There was a flow of water. Perdita washed her hair, and put it up in rollers. She asked Maggie for a razor to shave her legs and armpits. She covered her body with hormone cream. She pinched her neck all over. After some callisthenics she dressed, putting on a turtle neck, and looked as before.

Six o'clock came. There was no sign of Peter. Perdita never let on what she really felt. Pacing, she joked. Maggie mixed her one strong drink after another. She had never seen Perdita so ruffled.

Two hours later the bell went. Perdita opened the front door with her hair skewed over her brow. Keeping to her resolution she did not bawl him out.

Peter came in wearing a white suit, leaving an aroma of Chanel in his wake, Nordic and callow, he rarely spoke. He drank no alcohol, he had a mysterious liver complaint. Perdita tottered out into the street and bought him Vichy water from the delicatessen. She brought him the rest of the chicken. He was upset when a speck of salad oil fell on his suit. Perdita took it off with cleaning fluid. Every time one of the women brought out a cigarette Peter delved into his skin-tight pants and got out a gold lighter. Darting forward he flicked it. Each time Maggie expeced his fly to burst open.

He said he was mad at his mother, she'd thrown away his favourite suit, saying it was too worn. Maggie said she was planning to have her apartment painted. Perdita said it needed it.

Peter joined Maggie on the sofa. Couldn't he do it for her in his spare time. He'd much rather paint her walls than have to trail into an office every morning. Maggie thought it a good idea. Not liking the turn of events Perdita said they must go. At ten she took him home.

Maggie didn't see them for a month. One Friday evening Peter called. He was frantic. He said he had quit his job. He needed money. Could he do up the apartment? She need only pay him a minimal. Maggie agreed. She called Perdita, and told her.

Perdita had been drinking. 'It's all over,' she said, 'He's impossible. Expects me to throw all my clothes out to make room for his suits. Comes home at two in the morning. It's over . . .' Maggie consoled her. She was sure they'd make it up. 'Never . . . I'm not going to be a doormat.'

In the morning Maggie bought the paint. Peter came round in bursting jeans and a baby blue pullover. He looked forlorn. Perdita had thrown him out. He was in a hotel. He thought it was something to do with the constricted conditions in which they'd been living. 'Purdy's apartment's so small. Unlike yours . . .' A funny expression came over his face. Maggie understood. On the sofa she consoled him. After painting the kitchen Peter stayed the night.

'Is Pete there,' Perdita's voice said sternly, early next morning. 'Put him on to me.'

Getting into his jeans and baby blue pullover, he said,

'She wants me to go round and see her.'

He went back to Perdita. A month later he got a good job. He was to accompany a photographer to Europe to cover collections. He would be away a month. While he was away Perdita was going into a hospital to have a foot operation and a face lift. It would cost all of the two thousand dollars she had saved.

Only Maggie was allowed to visit her. Perdita's face was bandaged, and her long legs trussed up with the feet protruding from the end of the bed like swathed floor mops.

The day Perdita was due to hobble out she asked Maggie to come round after work and help her clean the apartment.

'I'm in fearful shape. After being in bed so long. I'll have to make a special effort with my exercises. We might go swimming at the Y.W. when the scars on my feet are less obvious.'

Perdita's door was ajar. The central heating was stifling.

'Hallo, Purdy,' Maggie said affectionately. Perdita gave her the camera flash smile that now seemed a trifle glassy. Her face was smooth and stunning. She was in black panties. She lowered a pair of dumbells, and pointing at Maggie's skirt said in a deploring shocked tone,

'Just look at your hem! I hope nobody saw you coming up the stairs.'

'The man on the first floor was practising a zither with his door open,' Maggie laughed, 'I've brought you some flowers.'

'Not marigolds! I don't know where I'm going to put them in all this mess.'

Maggie hadn't been to Perdita's for a long while. As she broomed she scanned the walls. In place of the photographs of celebrities taken by Perdita during a fleeting romance there now hung photographs of queers posed as women, and one of Perdita as a transvestite. Perdita had hired two abstract paintings on a monthly basis from the Museum of Modern Art in an effort to cheer up the place for Pete's return.

Maggie lifted the Spanish rugs and dusted under the pretty dim-lit Art Nouveau lamps while Sinatra droned. Perdita went on doing push ups. She washed her hair, and shaved her legs and armpits.

Perched on the bed she went through the grease pat ritual, rubbing hormone cream into her ankles and elbows. She pinched her neck. She followed it with a rose water dousing, meanwhile complaining of the way Maggie was disposing of the filth. Clothes were scattered all over. The closets were crammed. Since a year the overflow of suits had been packed into cellophane bags and hitched on to the empty book shelves covering one wall of the tiny room. Perdita planned to go through her clothes and get rid of anything she hadn't worn in a long while to create space for Pete's things.

'Not that light over there. For heaven's sake,' she said, as Maggie lit up the closet that passed for a kitchen. 'You've brought fish again?'

'How would you like it cooked?'

'Don't shout! Haven't I told you before. Don't shout!'

Maggie spread a cloth over the bedspread, and brought in the cutlery. 'Not those plates! I can't understand why I haven't heard from Pete. He was due back yesterday. He wrote a week ago, said he'd call as soon as he arrived.

Three times Perdita went downstairs and looked into the mail box, thinking the mail might have been delayed. She tested the bell to make sure it rang, in case a cable came. Absent-mindedly she carried a garbage bag three blocks and into the drug store.

They ate seated side by side on the bed. Perdita had put on her gloves. Maggie looked into the stunning smooth face with its drawn expression. Even her body was staggering.

'Why are you eating with your gloves on?'

Perdita took off the black gloves. Her beautiful eyes, the one real part of herself that remained, were desperate. She held up her hands. They were the withered hands of an elderly woman. She replaced her gloves and creepily picked up the fork.

'Nothing you can do about that. Nothing! A few more years and I'm going to swim out to sea and never come back.' She unhooked the receiver. 'If he rings now. He won't get me. I'm no doormat.'